Cedar Creek

Christmas at Cedar Creek
Snowstorm at Cedar Creek
Sunlight on Cedar Creek

Pine Harbor

Allison's Pine Harbor Summer
Evelyn's Pine Harbor Autumn
Lydia's Pine Harbor Christmas

Holiday House

The Christmas Cabin
The Winter Lodge
The Lighthouse
The Christmas Castle
The Beach House
The Christmas Tree Inn
The Holiday Hideaway

Highland Passage

Highland Passage
Knight Errant
Lost

Highland Soldiers

The Enemy

The Betrayal

The Return

The Wanderer

Highland Vow

American Hearts

Secret Hearts

Runaway Hearts

Forbidden Hearts

For more information, visit jljarvis.com.

LYDIA'S PINE HARBOR CHRISTMAS

LYDIA'S PINE HARBOR CHRISTMAS

PINE HARBOR ROMANCE BOOK 3

J.L. JARVIS

LYDIA'S PINE HARBOR CHRISTMAS
Pine Harbor Romance Book 3

Published by Bookbinder Press
bookbinderpress.com

ISBN (paperback) 978-1-942767-98-5
ISBN (ebook) 978-1-942767-99-2

ONE

THE SCENT of gingerbread wafted in from the kitchen of the Silva Brothers' Brewpub as Lydia, Christmas greenery draped over her arm, climbed a ladder. She merrily hummed along with a jaunty Christmas carol as she pressed an adhesive hook onto a beam and draped the last of the greenery over it. The repurposed-warehouse-turned-seaside-bar had been sufficiently transformed for the holiday season. With its view overlooking Pine Harbor, Maine, the place already had more than its share of seaside charm. Fresh evergreen garlands entwined with red ribbon surrounded the windows and wound around every overhead beam. Holly, strategically placed mistletoe, and wreaths bedecked with fairy lights completed the effect.

"There. How does that look?" She looked over at

Marco, but he was busy pouring a glass of wine for a pretty young brunette at the bar. The poor woman had the same dumbstruck expression Lydia had seen so many times. It was the look of a smart woman turned senseless by Marco's effortless charm. When it was combined with his manly square jaw, deep-set brown eyes, and dark wavy hair, he was irresistibly attractive. Of course, Lydia was biased, but she also had eyes. She couldn't fault the young woman for the look on her face. With practice, Lydia had learned to hide Marco's effect upon her, but she felt it nonetheless.

No woman had ever reduced Marco to a drooling, dumbstruck shell of a man. Lydia wondered what that might look like, yet she didn't want to see it because someone else would have prompted it. She sighed. It was pointless to ponder such matters. Marco wasn't looking for love. He breezed through life, blissfully unaware of his effect upon women. No doubt he was over there thinking he was simply doing his job, manning the bar and serving drinks while playing the sociable-bartender role. But for Lydia, moments like that served as a reminder that she and Marco were friends—good and reliable friends but most importantly platonic friends. She had always known it intellectually, but her heart needed frequent reminders.

"Hello? Lydia? I said that looks perfect!" came Allie's voice from below.

Lydia awoke from her reverie and climbed down the ladder. Side by side, she and Allie surveyed their handiwork. Neither spoke as they took it all in.

Finally, Allie said, "The windows and beams look fantastic. As for the rest, it's not nearly enough."

"No, not even close." Lydia had concluded that minutes before but had waited to hear Allie's thoughts. Allie was her boss and the owner of The Gallery, a gift shop in town, but she was at the brewpub on a personal mission. Theo Silva was also Allie's boyfriend. He'd mentioned in passing that he had no plans to decorate the bar for the holidays. Appalled, Allie emphatically offered to decorate the bar for him. She assured him it would be good for business, and of course, she was right. Even Marco leaned toward her side of the issue. Once Lydia agreed to help Allie, it was more or less a done deal. Theo had no strong feelings one way or the other, so if Allie and Lydia wanted to spearhead the project, he had no objections. As for Lydia, she was happy to help. Her feelings for Marco had nothing to do with it. It was a Christmas emergency. They had no other options. The Silva Brothers' Brewpub would have holiday cheer. If it meant spending a couple of afternoons in the same room as Marco, she would take one for the team.

Allie called, "Marco, we need your opinion." She lowered her voice so much that Lydia wondered if she was thinking out loud. "We've run out of greenery. I might have another box of ornaments back at the shop, but that's pretty much it."

Lydia studied Allie. "And Marco's opinion affects matters how?" Sure, Marco was a half owner—a tremendous accomplishment for someone so young. He had his older brother to thank for getting the business on its feet, but Marco was amazing at his job. Sometimes he looked more like a monarch holding court than a bartender serving drinks. Perhaps she was biased, but she recognized his flaws too. Lydia wouldn't trust the guy to match his own socks, so she was baffled by Allie's sudden interest in his decorating opinion. Theo was no better, unless the goal was to deck the place with sports memorabilia. Lydia could only imagine what that would look like. *Deck the halls with balls of volley, ball-la-la-la-la, la-la-la-la.*

Marco dried his hands on a bar towel and joined them. "What's up?"

Allie looked around helplessly, which made Lydia smile. Very little in life rendered Allie helpless, so she had to be up to something. "We're out of greenery."

That didn't make sense. If Allie was angling for

more money to buy decorations, she could easily have asked Theo. Unless he'd just snuck out the back door, Lydia was pretty sure Theo was in his office, which was just a short walk through the kitchen.

Marco took the greenery news well. "This looks amazing." He turned and looked back toward the bar, but before he could leave, Allie hooked her arm around his elbow. "This is only the beginning. Marco, when's the last time you got out for a good whiff of fresh air?"

He eyed her skeptically. "I took the trash out ten minutes ago."

She laughed. "But wouldn't it be fun to go strolling through the woods, gathering evergreen branches and twigs?"

His eyebrows drew together. "Frolicking through the woods isn't really my thing."

"Frolicking? I believe I said strolling. By which I mean hiking with your blue jeans tucked into a pair of good, sturdy boots and an ax resting on your plaid-flannel-shirted shoulder."

"So, like, a regular day." His eyes twinkled. "Look, Allie, why don't you work out this Paul Bunyan fantasy of yours with my brother. I'm not judging. What happens with you two stays with you two. I just don't want to know."

"Very funny! I just need some greenery to finish

decorating here. You may not be able to envision it now, but you'll thank me later. People want to see decorations at this time of year. It puts them in the holiday spirit."

"I've got a few bottles behind the bar that'll put people in the holiday spirit."

"Wrong spirit. Here's my dilemma. I've got some inventory coming in tomorrow, and I really have to be in the shop. So if you could gather some greenery, that would be a huge help."

Lydia tried not to smile as Marco's face took on a pained but polite expression. "What kind of greenery?"

Allie's eyebrows furrowed a little too much. "Oh, you know. Tell him, Lydia."

Lydia shot a look at Allie, who in turn did an excellent job of avoiding eye contact. That left Lydia to explain. "You know... evergreen stuff like you see on the trees and wrapped around... things at this time of year." She looked sideways at Allie.

Allie narrowed her eyes and appeared to be thinking. "You're not going to know what to get. No, you're going to need help, aren't you?" Before he could answer, Allie said, "Unfortunately, I'll be stuck at the shop." Her face brightened. "Oh! But Lydia here knows exactly what's needed."

Lydia forced a smile. *Allie, no. I know you're*

trying to help because you see me staring at Marco all the time, which I've really got to get better control of, but you're not helping me get over this hopeless crush, so...

"Lydia! Why don't you go with Marco? I can check my inventory while you gather all that we need to finish decorating the bar. Perfect! Problem solved."

Your problem, maybe, but you've just made mine worse.

Allie cast a purposeful look Marco's way. "Lydia will know just what I need, and you've got just the right muscles to get the job done." She smiled at Lydia. "I've got an old sled in the back of the shop. You could use that to drag the heavier branches and whatnot. We need enough to finish decorating the entrance, and we'll need some smaller bits for the table arrangements. Oh, and some pine cones would be nice. Make that a few dozen. I'll find some red ribbon—or red plaid, even better—and floral wire. Keep an eye out for some mistletoe, but just to be safe, I'll stop at the florist." She clasped her hands to her chest. "Oh, it's going to look so gorgeous in here!"

Marco seemed confused, but that was the least of Lydia's worries. She'd been counting on Marco to nix the whole thing, but he hadn't. The whole greenery-and-pinecone-gathering outing was beginning to look like a done deal. Lydia took a breath and prepared to protest, but Allie continued.

"The bar opens at eleven, so you'll both need to be out bright and early so that Marco can make it back in time for the lunch rush. How does seven o'clock sound?"

"How about eight?" Marco offered. Marco tossed a questioning look at Lydia, and she responded with a helpless shrug. Sounding resigned, Marco said, "Okay, I'll pick you up at eight. I'll bring coffee. I know how you are in the morning." He grinned then returned to the bar.

In disbelief, Lydia watched him walk away. *"I'll bring coffee?" Isn't it enough that he sets off my smart watch's health app cardio alarm? Does he have to be so thoughtful too?* It looked like they would be spending the morning together. So much for putting distance between them. It would be so much easier if he were a jerk or unbearably dull. Then it wouldn't matter how handsome he was. He would be easy to dismiss. But every moment she spent with him, as much as she enjoyed it, made her heart cry out for something that it could never have. They were never going to be more than friends.

Allie cleared her throat loudly. *Oh no. I was staring again, and she caught me.* Lydia did her best to appear nonchalant, which was futile since the damage was done.

But Allie was kind enough not to comment. Instead, she thrust a large cardboard box into Lydia's arms. "Careful. It's a little heavy. Would you mind taking this out to the car? I'm just going to duck into the office to see Theo."

"No problem." As Lydia headed for the exit, Marco called from behind the bar, "Need some help?"

A guy at the bar swiveled around in his bar seat. "I've got it."

Her eyes darted to Marco, who assured her, "It's okay. He's a friend. This is—"

"Bryce?"

Marco stared with surprise.

Yes, Marco, I know people.

Before she could explain, Bryce looked over his shoulder at Marco. "We're in the same Global History class. Here, let me help you with that."

Lydia wasn't sure, but she thought Marco's jaw might have gone a bit slack as Bryce practically leaped from his stool and took the box from her.

As they walked out to the car, Lydia looked up at Bryce. "You're a lot taller in person—I mean out of class."

"Really? Well, in class, I'm usually sitting at a desk."

"Yeah, right." She chuckled awkwardly. "What was I thinking?" *That you were tall and had brilliant blue eyes?*

"So, you and Marco..."

"Me and Marco...?"

He grinned. "How long have you two been together?"

"Zero... time." *Well said, Lydia.*

He looked surprised. "Oh. But I've seen you together a lot on campus."

"Yeah, we carpool. Sort of. Not really. He drives me to school."

"Oh, that's nice."

"Yeah, that's Marco. He's nice." *Really nice.*

Bryce looked satisfied enough with her answer to look straight into her eyes. "So are you."

"You don't even know me." *But who cares? You are excellent at making eye contact and—oh no, I'm blushing.*

"I'm a pretty good judge of character."

"I'm an ax murderer." Lydia didn't crack a smile.

Bryce burst out laughing. "You're funny."

Most people just laugh, but thanks for the explanation. Lydia tried not to furrow her eyebrows. She wasn't sure what to make of him.

They arrived at Allie's car, and Lydia tore herself away from his tractor-beam gaze long enough to open the hatch. He loaded the box and pulled down the hatch, then they stood for a moment in silence. It should have been awkward, but Lydia actually enjoyed it. That was new. A guy was completely focused on her, and she was only a little bit nervous. Bryce flashed a grin, as though he'd just come to his senses. "Well, see you Monday."

"Tuesday," she corrected.

"Oh, right. Global's a Tuesday-Thursday class."

Allie gave a sort of limp wave and said, "Bye." *What was that? 'Cause that was not even close to a wave. That was more like a flailing dolphin. Just when I thought I'd make it through one conversation without embarrassing myself. I just can't be around men. That's all.*

TWO

Lydia left with Bryce, leaving Marco trapped behind the bar and feeling left out. Bryce looked like a puppy in a park, chasing after a frisbee—if Lydia were brightly colored, plastic, and round. Marco wondered about his new buddy Bryce. He only knew him from school. They were in the same English Comp class, and more often than not, they hung out after class with a few other students—not so much from a thirst for knowledge as a thirst for the coffee shop in the building next door.

Bryce returned to his stool at the bar. "So, what's the story with Lydia?"

"Story?"

"Yeah. She's cute. What's her story?"

Yeah, she is cute. That's her story. The rest is none

of your business. "She's a local. We went to the same middle school and high school."

Bryson peered at Marco. "Oh, sorry. Are you… interested in her?"

Marco practically recoiled. "No. Why would you think that?"

"I don't know. I just got a vibe."

A vibe? With Lydia?

"I guess you must be pretty close friends."

"Yeah. I guess we are." *So hands off, loser. You don't deserve her.*

"Is she dating anyone?"

Bryce was really getting on Marco's nerves. He looked toward the end of the bar to see if he could use something as an excuse to get away from the guy. "No, she's not dating anyone."

"Good."

"Because Lydia doesn't really date."

Bryce seemed to find that amusing. "Why? What makes you think that? Because she won't go out with you?"

Is this guy deliberately trying to piss me off, or does he just have a gift? "No, because I haven't asked her."

"Hey, sorry. I guess I touched a raw nerve. You have feelings for her. Got it."

Bryce was way too sure of himself, so Marco refused to give him the satisfaction of being correct in his psychoanalysis. "My feelings for Lydia are... she's like a sister. No, more like a really close friend." He leveled a serious look at Bryce. "Close enough that I would hate to see anyone hurt her."

"Hey, don't look at me. I'm one of the good guys. I say please and thank you and help old ladies cross the street. Do you need references?"

That made Marco laugh, which helped ease the tension, at least on the outside. "No. You seem harmless enough."

"Hey!"

"Just kidding." *Not really. You're freaking annoying.*

Bryce grinned, pulled out his wallet, and tossed some bills onto the bar. "I've got to go. See you in class."

"Yeah, later." *Lydia and Bryce? Nah, she'd never go out with him.*

ALLIE PULLED out of the parking lot and headed back to the Gallery with Lydia, still deep in thought about Marco. "So, Allie, what was all that about?"

"All what? I don't know what you're talking about."

"Oh, I think you do."

Lydia launched into a theatrical reenactment of the moment in question. "Oh, Marco! Why don't you take Lydia here into the deep woods for some quality time?"

Allie stifled a laugh. "I don't think that's quite what I said or how I said it."

"Close enough."

"Sorry. I just think you two are so cute together."

Lydia nodded. "We are. We're adorable—adorable friends, which is all we'll ever be."

Allie had that look on her face she got when she was thinking of rearranging the shop, which was fine for the shop but not so fine for Lydia's life.

"I can't be misreading the signals. You two have chemistry—maybe not on the surface, but there's something there." Her voice trailed off as she looked over at Lydia.

Lydia considered whether to confide in Allie. Although Allie was more of her mother's friend—reason enough to exercise caution—she was Allie's friend too. But Allie was also her boss. Lydia decided that some things were better left unspoken—like her feelings for Marco.

Allie shrugged. "Well, I still need some fresh greenery to finish the brewpub. And we'll need votive candles and holders for the tables. Oh, and floral wire. I can get that when I pick up the mistletoe. We'll hang that strategically throughout the bar."

"I feel a sexual harassment lawsuit coming on."

Allie raised an eyebrow. "Do you mean to tell me that if Marco cornered you under some mistletoe, you'd sue him?"

"No, I'd sue you. Oh, look! Here we are! Thanks for the ride. See you tomorrow." Lydia hopped out of the car and rushed into her apartment, which was conveniently located next door to Allie's shop.

Once inside her room, she let down her carefree demeanor and thought about the new situation Allie had created. She knew about Lydia's feelings. That much was clear. How she knew was a mystery to Lydia, but she could think of no other explanation for Allie's sudden interest in playing matchmaker for them. She'd picked up on the chemistry, which was a polite way of describing Lydia's starry-eyed gaze fixed on Marco whenever she was near him. She was no Madame Curie, but chemical reactions didn't work just one way. That was what she had with Marco.

Allie knew her too well. What she didn't know was that for months, Lydia had been trying to let go of those feelings, but her heart wouldn't obey. She was trying so hard to get over Marco, then Allie had to butt in. Allie meant well, but she had just thrown fuel on the fire.

A whole morning with Marco—it was torture, yet she looked forward to it.

THREE

Marco parked his SUV at the end of a private road at the top of a hill. Lydia hopped out and met Marco at the back of the car.

As he opened the hatch, she said, "Are you sure it's okay if we trespass all over the place, taking evergreen branches from somebody's land?"

Marco smiled at her as if she were a child. "You worry too much."

"About trespassing? Yes, because as much as I love Christmas, I'd rather not go to jail for traipsing around someone's property and denuding the landscape."

Marco turned to face her and put his hands on her shoulders. Her heart skipped a beat, but she pulled it together. *We're just friends. There is nothing between us. My heart is not pounding. Nor am I aware of the gentle pressure of his fingertips on my shoulders or the way he is gazing straight into my eyes without saying a word. For God's sake, please stop. Do not part your lips.*

Marco blinked. He was frowning, as though he'd just awoken from a horrible dream. She'd just had a dream, too, only hers wasn't horrible.

He looked confused. "Sorry, I just..."

Had a nightmare? It was about me, wasn't it? I know. I get it.

"I, uh, was going to say that we have permission to be here. Theo's saving up for a down payment on this land. He's friends with the owner, so we're good."

"That's a relief. I had visions of an unkempt recluse emerging from a cabin—probably irate and possibly armed."

Marco peered at her. "So you're okay with a recluse who's fastidiously kempt?"

"Yes, and I'd probably date him."

Suppressing a grin, Marco said, "In that case, I'll keep an eye out."

"Thank you." She reached for the sled in the back of the car.

"Leave it. We should be able to find what we need within a short walk from the car. If that doesn't work out, we can come back for that later."

"What'll we use for the branches?"

He reached into the back and pulled out two enormous Ikea bags and gave one to her.

"That'll work." She turned toward the woods. "Which way?"

Marco pointed, and they were off on their evergreen adventure. As soon as they entered the woods, the smell of pine trees engulfed them.

Lydia took in a deep breath. "I thought Allie was nuts when she sent us out here, but it's gorgeous up here and so quiet and peaceful."

Marco's eyes lit up as he looked up at the trees. "I love it here. Theo and I have talked about building two cabins. With about a dozen acres to work with, there's plenty of room."

"That sounds perfect."

With a mischievous look in his eye, he said, "Perfect for what?"

Her mind took off on its own side trip as she thought about Marco living in his perfect little cabin in the woods, overlooking the ocean. All it was missing was her. And there she was again, back on her usual circuit in which her mind ran around a romance-laden track like a runner who didn't know enough to stop. Of course, the only exercise she got was in futility. She desperately wanted to be free, which was why hiking with him was such a bad idea.

"Hello? Perfect for what?"

"What? Oh. Cabin building. You could be a recluse-in-training. While you're at it, you could build a still, hide it from the revenuers, and supply the brewpub with your own moonshine in canning jars." Her mind wandered to thoughts of Marco shirtless in overalls—typically not her favorite look for a man, but for Marco, she could make an exception.

"That's an oddly thorough plan you've cooked up."

"I've got an oddly thorough imagination." *That is so sadly true.* With what must have looked like impressive enthusiasm, Lydia started gathering branches that had fallen in the last storm that blew through.

Marco took a more direct route by pulling out his band saw and cutting off some low-hanging branches. As if sensing her judgment, he said, "Don't worry. A little pruning won't hurt them."

They settled into a quiet routine of gathering branches and filling the bags on their shoulders then carrying them back to the car. As they emptied their second load, Marco said, "One more trip ought to do it, don't you think?"

Lydia thought for a moment. The last thing she wanted was to come up short and have to come back for more. If that happened, she would come back alone. "Yes, just one more bag each to be safe."

They headed into the woods in a new direction. To keep her mind from straying to Marco, Lydia concentrated on the rhythm of their boots crunching over the shallow coating of snow on the ground. When they had nearly filled their bags, Lydia bent down to pick up the last few branches she needed while Marco sawed off a few branches nearby.

With her bag completely stuffed, Lydia turned and headed toward Marco. "Are we ready to—*oof!*" Her foot caught on a tree root, and she went flying. Falling was an odd process. The bag took flight on its own while she grasped at the air as if it had the power to reroute her flight. It did not. She landed on Marco with enough force to take him down with her. Stunned, they both lay on a blanket of snow for several moments.

"Are you okay?"

"Sorry." Lydia scrambled off to the side, freeing Marco from the full weight of her body. She had almost forgotten a similar scene in her bedroom when he had climbed the tree outside her window to save her from herself, or so he'd thought at the time. *Why does this keep happening? Am I so desperate that I subconsciously created opportunities for full-body contact?* She couldn't really blame her subconscious. "I tripped."

"Yeah." He looked at her as if she had just said the most obviously ridiculous thing, which she had. Then he burst into laughter, and she joined him.

When the laughter subsided, she asked, "Did I hurt you?"

"You could never hurt me."

He'd meant it as a compliment. Lydia knew that. But it had another truth in it that caused a pang in her heart. She couldn't hurt him because he didn't feel enough for her to hurt. *You are reading way too much into this.*

Marco stood and held out his hand to pull her to her feet. "I think we've gathered enough for one day. I'll just top off my bag on the way to the car."

As they walked, Marco held on to her arm. "Just in case," he assured her, grinning.

That was the part that she hated. He was just being her pal Marco. *Why can't that be enough?*

The drive home was uneventful, unless one counted pining for the driver for a half dozen miles as eventful. He pulled into her driveway and parked.

"Thanks for the ride."

For some reason that Lydia couldn't quite pinpoint, Marco found that slightly amusing. But when he put the car in park and turned to her, the smile faded. Lydia had grown used to her tendency to blow every expression and gesture out of proportion where Marco was concerned, but that time, it was different. It was so slight that it was barely perceptible, but as he tilted his head, Lydia had the strangest sensation that he was seeing her differently. Whether that was a positive thing wasn't clear.

"What?" Speaking would break whatever spell seemed to have fixed his gaze on her, but she couldn't bear it any longer. That much uninterrupted attention was a powerful thing for a vulnerable heart to endure.

He smiled gently. "Bye, Lydia."

"Bye." She got out of his car and walked into her home, feeling as though something had changed. She didn't know what it was. That fact scared her a little because it made her feel closer to Marco, and closeness to Marco meant heartache.

FOUR

Lydia walked out of class into the gray haze of an early-December sunset. It was her birthday. When Marco had picked her up that morning, her mother invited him for some birthday cake after class. It was such a mom thing to do. At first, Lydia was embarrassed, but the idea grew on her as the day progressed. By the last class, she'd begun daydreaming of celebrating her birthday with Marco along with her mother and Dylan.

Her feelings toward Marco were like a pendulum swinging from avoidance to yearning. That day was the latter. She was glad to be spending time with him for her birthday. They had been through so much together that she hated to think her unrequited feelings would eventually cost her their friendship. She could only bear so much. But for the moment, time with Marco was always well spent with great talks and laughter. His friendship was almost enough, so having him join her for her birthday meant a great deal to her.

As she headed down the sidewalk, she searched for his old black SUV in the parking lot. It wasn't where he'd parked it in the morning, so she stood at the parking lot entrance and scanned the lot. Halfway down the first row of cars, she spotted his car. Smiling, she quickened her pace, but she stopped abruptly when a pretty young woman got out of the passenger side. Marco had a type—pretty, popular girls. They must have had other distinguishing features aside from their stunning good looks and starry-eyed gazes, though she'd never seen any. She wondered if he knew that women didn't flock to other men the way they did him. After all, that was his normal. He had an innate magnetism that drew women to him. She'd never seen anything like it.

Marco bounded around the car and arrived at the passenger side, where he leaned on the car roof as though he were sheltering the woman. Lydia could almost imagine what it would feel like to be sheltered like that. In the dusk, she couldn't make out their expressions, but the way she stood and leaned into him and the way Marco looked down at her appeared intimate enough to make Lydia uneasy about watching. Then he kissed her. Lydia started to turn. She could walk away and come back a few minutes later when the kissing was—she could only hope —over.

Marco glanced up with no warning. "Lydia!"

The woman turned and eyed Lydia from top to bottom.

"Lydia, this is Wendy."

Wendy, Wendy, Wendy. This time, I'll remember her name.

"Hi. Good to meet you." Lydia smiled pleasantly. She'd had plenty of practice.

Wendy squeezed his hand and left, which finally cleared the way for Lydia to get into the car and stare out the window. She hated herself for feeling what she was feeling. It had a name, but Lydia was determined to ignore it so that she wouldn't have to face it head-on. If she admitted she was jealous, it would mean all those feelings she'd been trying to bury had been waiting right there on the surface.

Marco got into the car and backed out of the parking spot. "So, birthday girl, have you had a good day?"

"Oh yeah, great!" *Until five minutes ago.* "So, Heidi's new."

His eyes darted toward her. "You mean... Wendy?"

Allie nodded vigorously, as if she'd meant to say that all along. "Yes. Wendy. She's nice."

"And smart. She got into three Ivy League schools but couldn't afford them, so she's going here for two years, then she's planning to transfer."

"Oh, that *is* smart." *So, now can I hate her?*

"Yeah. I'm lost in accounting, so Wendy's tutoring me."

With her tongue? "Oh, that's nice."

"We kind of got carried away."

"Strayed from the generally accepted accounting principles, did you?" *Come on, Lydia, acting snarky isn't becoming.*

"Yeah, she's got that look in her eyes, and I don't want to lose a good tutor."

Lydia leaned back and sighed. "Yeah, I hate it when that happens."

"You're judging me, aren't you?"

"No." *But yes, kind of.* "What's that look for?"

"It's a response to your look."

Lydia tried not to look defensive. "Which was?"

He lifted his eyebrows. "Disapproval."

"And your response?"

A moment passed. "I'm sorry."

He's serious. "What for?"

He gave her that soft, brown-eyed look that always, every single darned time, made her melt.

Sometimes she wondered if he did it on purpose. "For disappointing you."

"I wouldn't say disappointed." *No, it's more a matter of wishing I knew how to tutor accounting.*

Marco stopped at a light, which was good because his unwavering gaze would have gotten them into a wreck. She had two choices—gaze back until she got "that look" in her own eyes or look away and put herself out of her misery.

An unexpected plan C threw itself into the mix. Lydia laughed. "You are so easy." She pointed at him. "That's your conscience doing the judging. Hey, eyes on the road. The light changed." She grinned and mentally patted herself on the back.

He attempted a laugh, but his eyebrows wrinkled. "You'd tell me, wouldn't you?"

"Tell you what?"

"If you were disappointed?"

Probably not. "Marco, relax. You haven't done anything wrong."

And to her knowledge, he hadn't. Since she'd known him, Marco had done everything right. The guy drove her to and from school every day. Granted, he was going there too. But when things went wrong in her life, he was always there for her—as her friend.

Once home, they climbed the stairs to the

apartment she shared with her mother and opened the door.

"Happy birthday!" Her mother, Eve, and her mother's fiancé, Dylan, were there with a cake. Her mom was already lighting the candles.

It was nice. Lydia was lucky. She had people around her who loved her—or, in Marco's case, liked her. A card from her father, whom she'd only just met, lay on the counter. That was a sore subject with Dylan, so she would save that for later. For the moment, it was her birthday celebration, and she was happy.

Lydia blew out the candles, and as they ate the cake, Marco gave her a gift card to her favorite coffee shop.

She laughed. "You know I'll use this!"

His eyes sparkled. "I had an idea you might." He stretched out his arms. "Happy birthday."

They embraced. He was warm, and he felt really good—and her mother and Dylan were watching.

She pulled back a little abruptly. *Oh, this feels so weird. Although I ought to be used to that feeling by now.* "Thanks, Marco." She lifted the card and looked into his eyes then quickly averted her eyes as she smiled. She could only imagine how that smile had looked, because it felt like a kindergartener's portrait session—stunned, lips over teeth, and unnatural.

Dylan gasped and, looking way too surprised, said, "Oh, a present! We forgot! Oh no!" He frowned. At least her mother could rest easily, knowing that Dylan would never run off to Hollywood to become an actor. He was good-looking enough, for an old guy in his thirties, but acting—nope, not an option for him.

Eve said, "Follow me."

Lydia glanced at Dylan. Yeah, something was up. They all followed.

Then her mother stopped. "I forgot a blindfold."

Well, aren't we being dramatic?

Eve spotted Lydia's scarf. "That'll do."

She extended her hand, so Lydia gave it to her. They went outside, and Lydia discovered she wasn't a big fan of walking blindfolded among motor vehicles. But they eventually stopped.

"Okay, you can look now."

Lydia looked around. "You got me a parking lot for my birthday?"

She looked at Marco, but he shrugged and shook his head.

Eve held out a key.

"A car key?" Then it sank in. "A car key!"

Eve smiled. "It's yours." She extended her hand toward a shiny blue subcompact. "It's a few years old, but Dylan knows a guy, and he painted and detailed it, so it's almost like new." Her mother looked almost as happy as Lydia was. Then she added, "Now Marco won't have to drive you to school."

"Oh, great." Lydia felt like she'd been punched in the gut. "Lucky you, Marco!"

He gave her a gentle half smile. "I didn't mind."

Her mother said, "Happy birthday," then hugged her.

"Thanks, Mom." It was a fantastic gift—the best birthday gift she'd ever received. She could drive herself to and from school. But she was going to miss Marco.

Dylan said, "Why don't you two take her out for a spin?"

Lydia tightened her grip on the key. "Oh, I'm sure Marco needs to get back to the bar."

"I think I can spare a few minutes. Come on, let's go see what this baby can do."

The two guys were practically beaming with joy—not that Lydia wasn't thrilled with her car. She was. And she was glad Marco wanted to ride in her car. It was her birthday, and he was happy for her. She looked around, and her heart was so full. She had everything she could have hoped for her birthday. Her mother was happy with Dylan. They were almost a family. And Lydia had a father. She couldn't wait to open his card. And Marco was Marco. But that was the problem. She wouldn't think of that for the moment.

They got in, and she turned the key in the ignition. "Okay, here we go!"

THEY DROVE THROUGH THE TOWN. In the dark, all the Christmas lights glowed. Marco suggested they park by the water to take in the harbor lights. It was a magnificent sight at any time of the year, but at Christmas, it was especially magical.

Lydia kept the car idling while they leaned their heads back and soaked in the scenery. "I'm so glad this is home. I love it."

"And now you can come over here anytime you want."

"This is a great way to top off my birthday." She started to shift into reverse and head for home, but Marco stopped her.

"Let's stay here for a minute."

"Okay." That caught Lydia off guard.

Marco unbuckled his seat belt and turned, leaning his arm on the seat back. "I have an idea. It makes good sense financially."

"Okay." He was sounding oddly practical, which

wasn't exactly her first choice when parked before a scene so romantic that it made the heart swell.

"Well, I was just thinking."

"Thinking is good."

Marco's practical expression disappeared, and the old Marco returned with a grin. "I know!"

When he didn't continue right away, Lydia said cheerfully, "Well, good. Thank you for sharing."

"Wait. Hear me out."

The longer he took to say whatever it was he had on his mind, the more uncomfortable Lydia became. But that was her problem. She was always overanalyzing everything that he said or did, even though she knew it was not all about her. In fact, it was seldom about her.

Marco slipped off his shoes and put his feet up on the dashboard then clasped his hands behind his head.

"Comfortable?"

He tilted his head. "Leather seats would be nice."

Lydia started to give him a playful swat with the back of her hand, but he caught her wrist. An awkward moment followed while he loosened his grasp on her wrist and set her hand down gently. Lydia's heart did the weightless thing it always did when he touched her. *I am so hopelessly lost.*

Oblivious to Lydia's moment of crisis, Marco said, "I got used to riding together."

That made Lydia far happier than it should have. "Me too."

Marco touched the button and tilted the seat farther back to almost a full recline. "You know, we'd save money if we carpooled. Not to mention reducing our carbon footprint."

Lydia gestured toward Marco's feet on the dashboard. "If your feet weren't so big, we wouldn't have to worry so much about that."

"I know. That's why we need to act now." A smile teased the corner of his mouth.

"What kind of act?" *Because you really shouldn't talk about performing acts together when we're in a parked car with your seat horizontal.*

"Carpool."

"Carpool?"

Marco pressed the button and raised his seat back up to its original position. "Yeah. I'll take Mondays, Wednesdays, and Fridays. You can drive Tuesdays and Thursdays."

"But..." *That is not going to help me break free.*

"Okay, we can alternate Fridays." He nodded as though it were settled then smiled and leaned back while he lowered his seat back again.

Lydia couldn't help but smile. "Having fun?"

"Try it. It's like an amusement park ride."

"Marco, have you ever been to an amusement park? 'Cause I'm pretty sure it's more fun than this."

"Lydia, nobody has more fun than we do."

She smiled and lowered her seat back. "How could they?"

And that's why I'll wind up spending the rest of my life like my mother, alone and unloved—except even she has found love.

So have I. Too bad it's one-way.

FIVE

Lydia shoved her books into her book bag, slung it crosswise over her shoulder, and headed out of class. It was a crisp winter day but not so far below freezing that she couldn't enjoy her walk to the car. A light dusting of snow laced bare tree branches and sparkled in the setting sunlight.

"Lydia!" Running footsteps approached her from behind.

"Bryce. Hi, how are you?"

Color flushed his cheeks. "I'm good." He pushed his hair from his forehead. "I was wondering if you were busy."

"When? Now?"

"Yeah. I thought we might go grab a cup of coffee and maybe go for a walk and check out the Christmas decorations in the shop windows in town."

That sounded like such a nice, Christmassy idea. She couldn't imagine Marco ever coming up with that. *Strolling by Christmas decorations?* The thought made her smile, but then she thought of Marco and looked toward the car. It was her turn to drive. "I can't today. I'm carpooling with Marco, and I can't leave him stranded."

Disappointment crossed quickly over his face. "How about tomorrow?"

Lydia thought for a moment. "I guess so. But tomorrow is Marco's turn to drive, so I would need a ride home afterward. I'd drive separately, but Marco and I share a parking tag."

His face brightened. "Not a problem. I was planning on doing that, anyway. So, why don't we meet right here tomorrow? When is your last class over?"

"Four o'clock."

"Great. See you here at four." As an afterthought, he added, "If the weather is bad, we can meet inside the admin building over there. I'll find you."

"Okay, see you then."

Bryce smiled. He had a really nice smile. He headed back where he'd come from.

As Lydia headed for her car, she wondered, *Is this a date? It seems like a date.* But she still wasn't sure. She'd arrived at the ripe old age of eighteen having gone on three dates total—and those barely counted since she'd only gone on them out of desperation. Apparently, desperation was not a good foundation for a relationship, because those relationships had lasted the span of one evening. While not quite disasters, none could be called enjoyable, much less romantic. But Bryce was different. For one thing, he seemed to like her. That was new. And she could see herself liking him. *Imagine that—requited feelings. Weird.*

Lydia barely had time to warm up the car before Marco plopped into the passenger seat.

She pulled out of the parking lot. "How was your day?"

"Okay. How was yours?"

"Good. So, tomorrow—"

"I'm driving. Don't worry. I won't forget you." He grinned.

Just say it. It's not a big deal. "I've got a... thing after school."

"A thing?"

"Yeah. So I won't need a ride home."

"Whoa. Hold on there. Back up. Not literally— keep driving. Explain."

Lydia kept her eyes on the road, but she could feel him staring at her.

"Come on. Out with it."

"Out with what? I'm... meeting someone for coffee." When Marco was silent, Lydia cast a quick sideways look then wished she hadn't. Rolling her eyes, she said, "It's just coffee."

"Just coffee?"

"And Christmas window-shopping in town—to look at the displays."

As if life's greatest truths had just revealed themselves to him, Marco said, "Oh! So you're meeting a girl."

That annoyed her so much that she wished she weren't driving. "Now, why would you say that?"

"Because what guy would ask you to go looking at shop windows?"

"Oh! So all guys should be exactly like you? Because they're not!"

"Okay! Sorry! Wow. I guess I touched a raw nerve."

"No, I just think your philosophy's a little off."

"Philosophy? I didn't know I had one."

"There's Marco's way, then there's the wrong way."

"That's not true. How many times have I listened to you and agreed?"

That was a good question for which she had no answer. "I don't have a counter. I should really get one. There must be a phone app."

"The answer is a lot. And I listen to Theo and Allie—lots of people. It's just that, in this case, trudging along icy sidewalks to look at shop windows wouldn't have come to my mind as an ideal first date."

"I didn't say it was a date. It's coffee. You and I have had coffee." *And I can regretfully attest to the fact that none of those coffees were dates.*

Judging from his silence, she figured that Marco had run out of objections.

Lydia pulled into the Silva Brothers' Brewpub parking lot to drop Marco off.

Only then did he ask her, "Who is it?"

"Bryce." *There, I've said it. It's out in the open. So why do I feel like I've just confessed to cheating? On whom?*

Marco looked as though he'd bitten into a lemon. "Bryce Rumsey?"

"Yes."

"You're going out on a date with Bryce Rumsey?"

"Not a date."

"That's right, it's—"

They both said, "Coffee."

He nodded knowingly. "And how do you know you can trust him?"

"Because we're taking a class together. He's a nice guy. We have friends in common."

"Oh? What friends?"

"Well, you, for one."

"I wouldn't call him a friend. We're in one class together. I've known him for a few weeks, which means basically nothing."

Nothing she could say would wipe the skeptical look from Marco's face where Bryce was concerned. "And what about you? How did you meet the last woman you went out with? Did you do a background check on her? Get references? Run a credit check? Women love that. Hi, my name's Marco. I see you've listed receptionist as your primary job. So this bank job, is that just part time? Oh, I see, you were only the getaway driver. Okay, how 'bout I pick you up at seven?"

He held up his palms and begged her to stop. "Okay, I get it. But it's different with guys."

"So what am I supposed to do? I mean, I thought about becoming an Anchorite monk, but then I found out they won't let you out for coffee and window shopping, which brings us back to—"

"What's an Anchorite monk?"

"Never mind. My point is you can't lock me up—"

Eyes ablaze, Marco said, "I wasn't suggesting that!"

Lydia was taken aback by his obvious frustration. "I didn't mean you personally. I just meant that life is a risk.

You're right. Bryce could be a horrible person, as could every man I ever go out with for the rest of my life. But you can't say that I'm not selective. I've been on exactly three dates in my whole life, so it's not like I've kicked up my heels and gone wild. Would you rather I didn't date at all? Spend my whole life alone? Because that's not what I want. I'd like to be cared for. I've got a right to be loved." *Oh. That was probably too much information.*

Marco looked stunned. *And why wouldn't he?* She had just vomited her emotions all over everything, and it wasn't pretty.

"I'm sorry. You're right. I'm being too overprotective." His eyes filled with warmth.

That softhearted expression made her forget her frustration with him. "I'm sorry, too—for unloading on you."

Marco grinned as though that were an understatement. "Go ahead. Go on your date."

"It's not a date!"

"Coffee. Have fun." He leaned over and gave her a kiss on the cheek.

Why does he have to do that? It was warm and tender. It was brother-like, but she didn't feel much like a sister.

"I'll see you in the morning." He got out of the car, but before he closed the door, he leaned down and said, "But I'm still going to do a background check on him."

"Marco!"

He turned and, without looking back, waved and walked inside.

IN SPITE of Marco's efforts to burst her dating bubble —efforts that included presenting her with a background check upon picking her up the next morning—Lydia went out with Bryce. And it went well.

Over coffee, they chatted about all sorts of things. He was easy to talk to and had a good sense of humor. While they talked, Lydia did a thorough study of his blue eyes, sandy hair, and strong jawline. He was taller than Marco by at least an inch, maybe two, and his hands were well-formed, with long fingers and remarkably well-manicured nails. She could see him ten years in the future, walking out of a bank in his topcoat and suit then stepping onto a commuter train to go home to his house in the suburbs.

After coffee, according to plan, they strolled down the street and looked at the shop windows, remarking on and laughing at things that they saw. Then they arrived at a small park by the main street that was used every winter as an ice-skating rink. A kiosk stood at the far side of the pond, where ice skates could be rented for a modest amount.

Bryce grabbed her elbow. "Come on. We've got to."

"Do you know how to skate?"

"Ten years of hockey. I played through high school, so yes. How about you?"

"I took a few figure-skating classes, but I could never manage to spin or skate backward. It became too embarrassing, so I moved on to something I could manage."

"And that was...?"

"Needlework."

"I'll bet you're amazing."

"Oh, I am! If needlework ever makes the Olympics, I'm in." She laughed. "I could teach you."

He grimaced. "No thanks."

"I taught Marco to crochet." She smiled as she recalled the two of them leaning over the counter in the Gallery while she taught him the chain stitch. He was so fun to watch because he took it so seriously.

Bryce's face appeared stuck in a grimace. "I'll leave the knitting to Marco."

"Crocheting."

"Whatever. Let's skate."

"Okay, but prepare to watch me fall—more than once."

"You won't, because I'll catch you."

She could hardly turn down an offer like that, especially with those blue eyes shining at her. "Okay."

He took her hand, and they ran to the kiosk. Ten minutes later, they were laced up and skating. As promised, whenever she started to falter, he caught her. Moving forward, hand in hand with him, Lydia was struck by the strangest sensation. They were having fun. She was on a date, feeling happy and carefree, with none of the usual angst that she felt when she'd gone out with others, especially Marco. Not that any time she spent with Marco could be classified as a date, but she wished that it could. Being with Bryce was different. They were so entirely at ease with each other, and Lydia thought she could enjoy getting used to the feeling.

An hour later, they turned in their skates, and Bryce took her home. They sat parked outside Lydia's apartment and talked until the windows fogged up.

Lydia said, "I better go in before my mother gets the wrong idea."

Bryce smiled gently and said, "I don't know about the wrong idea. It seems like a good idea." Then he leaned closer and touched his lips to hers. They were soft, and his kiss was so gentle and nice that Lydia couldn't help but smile as they parted.

"See you at school."

"Bye."

He waited until she closed the apartment door behind her, then she heard him drive off. After a quick climb up the stairs and a hasty hello to her mother, she went to her room, then she collapsed onto her bed and stared at the ceiling. Maybe Bryce was her chance. Maybe she would finally get over Marco.

MARCO HURRIED to finish his shift at the bar then went upstairs to study, but for a long while, he stared at his phone. It was none of his business how Lydia's date had gone. *But what if she's lying in the gutter somewhere?* Sure, Bryce looked okay on paper, but Marco still wasn't sure he bought Bryce's whole nice-guy act. Someone needed to check and make sure Lydia was okay. Of course, her mother would notice if she didn't come home. But her mother could be out with Dylan and have no idea her daughter was in trouble. He doubted Lydia had even told her mother that she had a coffee non-date. Marco was the only one in a position to save her if she needed saving. If something happened, Marco would never forgive himself for not having checked up on her. So that was that. It had to be done.

MARCO: *Are you still alive?*

    Lydia: *Very.*

    Marco: *Where are you?*

    Lydia: *Home.*

    Marco: *Good.*

    Lydia: *Did you need something?*

    Marco: *No, I'm good.*

    Lydia: *Me too. See you tomorrow.*

    Marco: *You're driving.*

    Lydia: *I know.*

    Marco: *Okay, bye.*

    Lydia: *Bye.*

MARCO SWIPED AWAY the text window. *Very alive? What's that supposed to mean?*

SIX

MARCO WAS STANDING OUTSIDE, ready to go, the next morning when Lydia picked him up. He realized he might appear overly eager to see her, but he couldn't help it. He was. Marco couldn't seem to shake the tendency to cringe every time he thought about Lydia's date the previous night. Not wanting to make matters worse, he had promised himself that he wouldn't make an issue of it. He got in and put a coffee in her cup holder.

"What's this?"

"What does it look like? It's coffee."

She practically sang, "That was so nice of you! Thanks!"

Marco frowned. "Relax. It's just coffee."

Lydia laughed. "I *am* relaxed. I just thought it was nice. You're nice."

"You're... in an awfully good mood." *I wonder why.* That made him cranky.

"Am I? I guess because it's the last day of final exams before Christmas, it's the start of winter break— and it's a new day."

Marco practically spit out his coffee. "You have got to be kidding me! You are not a morning person! Who are you, and what have you done with my friend?"

She gave him a disapproving sideways glance, but instead of answering him, she started humming along with the music on the stereo.

"That sounds festive." *Did I say festive? I meant insipid.* "I don't think you've played this before."

She gave the same light, carefree smile she'd had on her face all morning. *Why does that annoy me so much?* Then she said, "Oh, I don't know what it is. This is Bryce's Christmas Spotify playlist. He shared it with me."

"Oh." *Well, isn't that just adorable. I hate that carol... and singer... and, obviously, Bryce's taste in music.*

He decided that talking just wasn't going to work, so he folded his arms and stared out the window. *Sharing playlists. It must be true love.* Marco suddenly felt ill. *It* could *be true love.* He had never thought about Lydia falling in love. She was just Lydia, his friend. That Lydia would never have fallen in love and left him behind all alone. *No, you're overreacting. It was only one date. Get a grip. Be a man.*

Lydia parked the car and turned to face him. "Are you okay?" She looked genuinely concerned.

"Why wouldn't I be?"

"I don't know. You kind of look like you've just seen a ghost."

Marco tried to look cheerful. "Really?" He chuckled weakly. "No, I'm fine." He glanced at his watch. "I'd better get going."

"But we're a few minutes early."

Crap. She's right. Uh... "I've got an exam, and I need to study my notes."

Lydia looked a little confused. "Okay. Good luck."

"With what?"

"Your exam." Her confused expression intensified.

"Oh, right. Thanks!" Marco hopped out of the car and headed quickly to class. Maybe he *had* seen a ghost. *The ghost of Bryce-mas future.*

ALL MARCO NEEDED WAS a little time and space, so he took a few days off from Lydia. He had dealt with that dynamic before, only the roles were reversed. Of course, he and Lydia weren't dating. It was nothing like that at all. But he kept wanting to reach out for more time and attention than she seemed inclined to give him. The relationship was out of balance, and he couldn't help it. That was a red flag that something was wrong.

It was time for some space, and if past experience bore out his expectations, it would mark the beginning of something he called the drifting. Far subtler and kinder than ghosting, it resembled the downside of a relationship bell curve. Scheduling conflicts would crop up, then a private message might be left unanswered until the next day. Voicemail messages would be lost then phone calls ignored. There would be no emotional break. They would simply drift away from each other like a slowly peeled-off adhesive bandage. What distinguished it from past experiences was that Lydia would be the drifter and he the one being drifted from. He doubted she would even do it intentionally, but he saw it coming. It might be best if he preemptively put distance between them for a while. He needed to get her off of his mind. After Lydia worked through her Bryce phase, they could return to the way things used to be.

By Friday, Marco was feeling himself. Once again confident and in control, he was ready to face an unavoidable weekend together. It was the weekend of the town's annual Christmas market, in which local merchants set up booths full of gifts, food, and other magical Christmas delights. For the Silva Brothers' Brewpub, theirs was the magic of beer, and the booth next to theirs would house Allie's gift shop, the Gallery, where Lydia worked. Marco and Theo spent Friday afternoon setting up their booth and installing three kegs and taps along with an impressive display of their own bottled craft beers. Allie shared some of her evergreen garlands to decorate the brewpub's booth.

Things were shaping up beautifully until Lydia arrived. Marco thought he had sufficiently braced himself for a weekend an arm's length away from Lydia. But seeing her after a few days apart brought a sinking feeling he fought hard to shake. It was a good thing, he reasoned. He had had a few days to recover from his recent obsession with her. It was merely a test, and he had recovered. He'd been attracted to women before and had always gotten over them.

Marco stopped in his tracks. *An attraction? Who said anything about an attraction?* All the balsam fir scent was affecting his brain. He shook it off and got back to work.

When they finished setting up both of their booths, Theo stood beside Allie, admiring their work. "Why don't you come over for dinner?"

"That sounds great!"

Of course, he meant Lydia too. That was great. Just great.

They locked up the booths and all headed over to the Silva Brothers' Brewpub. Knowing they would be busy at the Christmas market, Theo had staffed up for the weekend. Taking advantage of the situation, he decided they'd earned a meal off-duty. So the four of them sat in the midst of the candlelit Christmas magic that Allie and Lydia had created, and they dined.

Lydia's hair was twisted into a knot with strands falling down here and there. For someone who had been working all day, she looked awfully cute. Messy hair was a good look for her, and the candlelight was a little bit dangerous. It was the kind of soft lighting that could confuse a guy prone to such things, but Marco was stronger than that.

Theo and Allie carried the conversation for the first several minutes, but a lull settled over the table, and Marco felt the need to fill in the void.

"So, how's Bryce?" He blurted it, then he wondered where it had come from.

Lydia's eyebrows drew together. He couldn't quite tell whether it was confusion or a hint of annoyance in her eyes. "He's fine."

"That's good."

Lydia eyed him suspiciously. "Is it?"

Okay, that was annoyance. Taking his cue from her reaction, Marco backed off and stopped talking.

By MORNING, the mood between them had thawed, no doubt aided by the steady flow of customers that kept both booths busy. Christmas music played throughout the market, and the weather, although cold, cooperated with clear, sunny skies. Even Marco was beginning to feel the holiday spirit. When Theo suggested they all get lunch from a barbecue booth a few aisles down, Marco volunteered to go pick up their order.

When it came time to take Lydia's order, she said, "Oh. No thank you, nothing for me."

Marco said, "You've got to eat."

She averted her eyes. "I've got other plans."

He raised an eyebrow then turned to take care of a customer.

Shortly after Marco returned with the lunch, Theo and Allie ducked behind their awnings to eat, and Bryce appeared at Lydia's booth.

"I'm on duty for a few minutes more." She said it quietly, but Marco had stepped outside of the booth to readjust the garland placement, which happened to place him in an optimal location for overhearing. It couldn't be avoided.

Bryce, as cheerful as always, said, "No problem. I'll just check out some of this craft beer next door."

Great. Five minutes of tortured politeness followed, during which Marco answered far too many questions about craft beer. For a guy who didn't brew his own, Bryce had an unnatural interest in hops. Marco had just about lapsed into a coma when Allie and Theo returned from their lunch break. Bryce quickly bought a four-pack of beer, left it in Lydia's booth, then swept her away for an enchanting Christmas ramble through the picturesque market. Meanwhile, Marco ducked behind the booth, sat on a cooler, and scarfed down his lunch all alone.

That gave him time to himself to think through the whole Lydia thing. He'd been so busy all morning with customers that he hadn't been able to. She and Bryce looked happy together, which should have been good for Lydia. She deserved to be happy. *If Bryce makes her happy, who am I to object?* Yet he did. In so many areas of her life, Lydia had excellent taste. She'd chosen Marco as a friend, for one thing. But Bryce wasn't quite up to par. Marco couldn't say why. He just felt something was off.

After analyzing the situation from all angles, he concluded that he was just being overprotective, like any brother would be. Still, he would keep an eye on Bryce. Someone had to, since Lydia's mother seemed to be asleep at the wheel. She was too much in love herself to see beyond her rose-colored glasses to what was really going on with her daughter. Or perhaps she was just happy to see Lydia dating. Marco had never known her to date—not that she couldn't have. She'd mentioned something about dating, but that was way in the past. There was nothing to keep her from dating. She was cute, smart, and more fun to be with than anyone else in their small community. Her problem was that she was too good for anyone that might have shown interest in her. She deserved someone special—which Bryce was not. That guy had his work cut out for him just to make the cut into average.

By the time Marco finished his lunch, he had determined that the best course of action would be to step back from Lydia's life, which, come to think of it, had already been the plan. She didn't need two men in her life, and besides, Marco had become way too closely involved. In doing so, he had broken his own rule where women were concerned—not that Lydia was a woman. Well, she was, but she wasn't a woman he was involved with, at least not romantically. They were friends. *Why is this starting to get so confusing?*

Bryce and Lydia returned from their lunch date

hand in hand. *Don't they look precious? Ugh.* Marco busied himself rearranging the stock while Theo rang up a customer. Unfortunately, he could only do so much work in a tiny beer kiosk also manned by his brother, so he managed to stay well aware of what was going on next door. Apparently, more people liked buying beer than buying art and needlework, because the Gallery's booth had enough of a lull for Bryce to lean over the counter, chin on hand, and chat up Lydia. *Isn't she on the clock?* She must have some work to do. But Allie seemed unperturbed. She was too easy on her employee. If it were up to Marco, he would have sent the guy packing.

After what felt like hours but was, according to Marco's watch, twenty minutes, Bryce finally left. That guy needed a hobby. He had too much time on his hands.

Almost immediately after Bryce left, the two booths were deluged by post-lunch shoppers and latecomers. By the time it let up, it was almost time to close for the day. Not much was left to do after Marco had used the excess energy he'd whipped up from his irritation with Bryce to get things in order. Allie and Lydia locked up their booth almost as quickly.

Theo and Allie would have plans, of course, which meant they would all have to walk out together.

Lydia walked beside Marco in silence until they were nearly at the entrance gate. "Marco, what's wrong?"

He hadn't expected directness. In truth, he had assumed she was blissfully unaware of his state of mind. "Nothing's wrong. I've just been working all day."

"Oh really?" She mocked him, sweeping her hand over her forehead for dramatic effect, and whined, "A whole day of work. That must be so hard." Just in case he couldn't tell she was being sarcastic, she seemed to feel the need to roll her eyes to drive home the point.

For all of the thought he had put into the situation, the best response he could come up with was a shrug.

Lydia stared for a moment then shook her head. "If this is what you're like after one day of working the Christmas market, I can't wait to see you tomorrow."

"Yeah? Well, I can't wait to see you either." *Brilliant retort. I guess you showed her!*

"Why, Marco! I didn't know you cared." She was toeing the line between sarcastic and bitter.

But Marco didn't fall into her trap. He hit her straight on with a bold comeback. "Well, I do!" *Dammit. That's not what I meant.*

On the plus side, that left her speechless, but it was only for a couple of moments. "Wow. Sorry I asked."

Marco narrowed his eyes. "But you did. You couldn't just let it go and ignore my bad mood."

Lydia's eyes clouded over. "No, because I care about you too. I know something's wrong. Asking was just a formality."

He was in no mood for that edge to her voice. "Well, now that we've dispensed with the formalities, I think we're done here."

If only they hadn't had another fifty yards to walk before they reached their cars. Apparently, it took a long time to walk that distance in total silence.

Lydia shortened the misery by lifting her chin and speed-walking away. Without turning back, she called, "Allie, I'll be in the car."

It was a strong exit, until she arrived at the car and discovered it was locked. While she tried all four doors, Marco bit his lip and barely managed to suppress his amusement. Allie was too busy laughing at something Theo had said to notice Lydia's dilemma. That was when Lydia unwittingly used her secret weapon. Seething, she folded her arms, crossed her legs, and leaned back against the car. Lydia was pouting. Marco couldn't resist smiling. He couldn't stay annoyed when she looked so adorably furious. It almost made the rest of the day's aggravation worth it. Almost.

SEVEN

WITHOUT MARCO'S KNOWLEDGE, the plan had been made for them all to go back to the bar and have dinner. Lydia had ridden with Allie, and Marco lived and worked there, so neither had a way out.

As they sat down to dinner, Marco said, "I'm surprised Bryce isn't here. Where is he—out curing cancer this evening?"

Lydia gave him a wry look. "No, he did that after lunch. What did you do?"

Theo and Allie stopped talking.

I thought about you. "Excuse me. Mel looks like she could use some help at the bar."

Marco arrived at the bar to find a total of three people with full drinks in hand, but the bar was the best place for him at the moment. He chatted with Mel for a minute then went to the back for some beer to fill the already-full cooler. Before he could pick up a case, he heard footsteps behind him.

"Theo, leave me alone."

"Wow, I need some new shoes if these make me sound like Theo."

Marco shut his eyes for a moment then turned around. "Allie, I'm fine. It's nothing to worry about."

"I know you're fine, but Lydia isn't. What's the matter with you? She won't give you the satisfaction of showing it, but you've hurt that girl's feelings."

Marco turned around with every expectation of hiding his feelings from Allie, but one look in her eyes, and he knew she'd seen through him. How she'd managed to figure it out was beyond him, since he had only just figured it out himself.

"Oh," she said as if he had just bared his whole soul.

"Oh what?" He needed to deny it, yet he couldn't. That would be lying, and lying to her would be almost like lying to Theo. He just couldn't do it. Instead, he exhaled and met her knowing look with what must have been sadder eyes than those of a whimpering puppy.

"Does she know?" Then she answered her own question. "Of course not. Otherwise, she'd understand instead of sitting out there feeling like she's just lost her best friend—which you are. Marco, you've got to tell her how you feel."

Eloquent genius that he was, Marco just shook his head. He couldn't even form words.

"So, you're just going to leave things like this?"

"I don't know." He had said words. That was progress.

Allie was speechless next, but she rallied soon enough. "Well, you've got to do something sooner rather than later, or you'll lose a friend who cares deeply about you."

"Don't you think I know that? Just what would I say? I barely understand what's going on myself, so how could I explain it to her? I just need some time to work through this."

"Okay. But it's not going to blow over like some sort of nor'easter."

"It may as well be. It's already blown through and destroyed everything that we had."

"So you rebuild."

"Allie, I know you're trying to help, but the only way you can help us right now is by not telling Lydia."

"Marco, you're asking a lot. She's not just my employee. She's my friend."

"Then as her friend, don't tell her anything. If I don't even know what to tell her, involving yourself will only confuse things."

"So I'm supposed to stand by and watch her suffer?" When Marco offered no alternatives, Allie sighed. "Okay. I won't say anything—for now—but I won't be happy about it."

"I can live with that."

She touched his arm. "Don't wait too long."

The door swung closed behind her, and Marco let out a sigh of relief.

MARCO RETURNED TO THE TABLE. He had to. He'd been absent too long, which would only make things more awkward. So he intercepted Mel as she brought out their dinner then took it over to the table and served them. That kept him busy enough to keep them distracted. He managed some small talk, which at least broke the tension. Mel stopped by the table a few minutes later to check how dinner was. After that, much to Marco's relief, Allie and Theo began talking about various Pine Harbor holiday events. Marco even managed to throw in a comment or two just for show, but Lydia remained almost entirely silent.

After what felt like a very long meal, Allie and Lydia left. As soon as they were out the door, Theo said, "What's wrong with you?"

"Can you handle the bar?"

Despite looking thoroughly puzzled, Theo said, "Yes."

"Good." Marco went upstairs and closed the door to his room.

What is wrong with me? That was an excellent question. The short answer was "a lot." Allie had figured it out, and he was pretty sure that his brother knew something was up.

Marco had feelings for Lydia. He should never have allowed it to happen. The only reason he'd let himself get close to her was that they were just friends. If they had been dating, he would have ended it by now. But their friendship had meant something to him, so he had allowed it to deepen, and he was in over his head. He thought back and tried to pinpoint when things went so desperately wrong.

Lydia had taught him to crochet. That alone should have been a red flag. If anyone else had suggested it, he would have told them what they could do with their yarn balls and hook. Maybe Lydia's crochet hook was enchanted and invisibly wrapped around his neck. There were crazier explanations for what was happening to him.

From there, things progressed to their brief life of crime—hacking into Decker's real estate presentation. Until then, Marco's impression of Lydia had been of a quiet schoolmarm type who strictly followed the rules.

But she had jumped right in and committed to the project, whatever the cost, and he loved her for that— not loved, liked. He just liked her as a friend and a partner in crime.

He smiled as he recalled the moment Theo had caught them red-handed, made them confess, then assigned what he thought was an appropriate punishment. Theo's version of community service was cleaning the toilets in the brewpub. It wasn't the sort of thing Marco would have expected to laugh his way through, but that was what they'd done. It was gross, but they had gloves and masks—that was Lydia's idea —and they laughed about it as they got the job done. Lydia made up a competition that involved dividing the bathroom in half and competing for speed and quality. They were about to ask Theo to judge when he interrupted and granted them both a reprieve.

Maybe that was what had cemented their friendship. If two people could enjoy cleaning a restaurant bathroom, they could conquer the world. Whatever the glue was that bound them together, from that day on, they remained close. After that, an hour didn't go by without them messaging one another. It was effortless then. *Why can't we just go back to that window in time?*

But what sent them over the line was the day they went searching for Lydia's father. She would have gone there alone, but she looked so vulnerable that Marco didn't hesitate. He knew he had to protect her. He still felt that way. Yet he had just hurt her feelings. She didn't deserve that.

He pulled out his phone and sent her a text. *Sorry. I'm a jerk. Bad day. Bad mood. Sorry.*

And you think that's enough?

I was hoping. He waited. Maybe she wasn't really angry with him, but he'd caught her at a bad time. He waited five more minutes. *Lydia?*

Marco tried periodically throughout the evening but was rewarded with silence. *Okay, I guess that means she's angry.*

EIGHT

MARCO LOOKED at himself in the rearview mirror as he sat in the parking lot behind the Gallery. *Today's a new day, and things always look brighter in the morning—for the sun. I'm not so sure about you. In fact, you look like a guy who hasn't slept, which sounds about right.*

He was stalling. Lydia had her lunch break in two minutes, so he didn't have much time to waste. He drew in a deep breath. It wasn't going to be easy, but it had to be done. So he sucked it up and got out of the car.

When he walked into the shop, he noticed a pair of gray-haired women within earshot of the counter, where Lydia stood scanning a box of new notepads. She glanced up with her pleasant shopgirl expression then, seeing it was Marco, shifted to a narrow-eyed look that nearly made Marco shiver. It was going to be a steep uphill climb. She averted her eyes, first looking at the customers then at random points in the shop—anywhere but at Marco. He pretended to examine various items as he casually browsed. He was actually skulking, which wasn't his style at all. But feeling that way wasn't his style either. This was just too darned uncomfortable.

With nothing to do but wait for the customers to make a decision and leave, he relived the highlights of his sleepless night. For some reason, Lydia's new boyfriend annoyed him. That had cost him thirty minutes of sleep right there. But for twenty more minutes, he thought of how happy she seemed with Bryce. That was twenty minutes he could have been sleeping. He pondered the pertinent question of whether his dislike for Bryce was significant enough to justify interfering with Lydia's happiness. Sometime during that mental debate, he realized what he wanted was irrelevant. Dating Bryce was Lydia's choice. She had the right to choose what made her happy, even if it made Marco unhappy. And unhappy he was—profoundly and miserably—enough to wallow in it until he drifted to sleep. Two hours of sleep was all he had left, and it had to be enough to get him through the day.

When he finally slept, Marco did not dream of Lydia. That would have been more than he deserved. Instead, he awoke with her name on his lips and the knowledge that he did indeed like her. It was as much of an epiphany as Marco had ever had. But liking Lydia was fine—or it ought to have been. They had been friends for months. Of course he would like her. But a friend would have been happy for a friend who found romance, because friendship and romance were two separate things. Friends didn't feel threatened by romantic entanglements. *So why am I?* No, that wasn't it. He didn't feel threatened. He was far too secure to give in to such weakness. Bryce meant nothing to him. It was Lydia he cared for.

Marco's stomach sank. Lydia meant something to him—more than something. But Lydia liked Bryce. Marco's chest ached. Lydia's feelings for Bryce bothered Marco because Marco's feelings for Lydia weren't feelings of friendship. Marco was jealous. That revelation was followed by an hour or more of denial, by which point he dozed off and slept just long enough to wake up feeling wretched.

In some ways, it didn't feel real. He might have blown everything out of proportion. In which case, seeing her in the plain light of day might resolve the whole problem. His new feelings might have lifted like the morning mist rising from the harbor. He had to be sure, and waiting wasn't an option. If he waited, these affectionate feelings might grow out of control. That was when he decided he had to see Lydia.

Theo, whose thoughts were focused on the upcoming lunch rush, said, "No." But Marco reminded him that he was an equal partner, which meant he didn't need Theo's permission. "Mel can handle it." Which she could, but that didn't mean she would enjoy it. It was amazing how much not enjoying she could convey with one look, but she did.

Marco gave her his most charming look, which he could tell from her response had lost its magic. He upped the ante. "I'll cover your next shift." All that got him was a blank stare. "And pay you for it, of course."

She perked up a little. "Okay." Then she turned and got on with her work.

Which brought him to his next mental state and location, fraught with conflicting emotions and parked behind Lydia's workplace.

ALLIE breezed in from the back room. "You can go take your lunch now." Then she looked up with a far more pleasant look of surprise than Lydia had offered him moments before. "Marco, hello! I didn't know you two had plans. Go ahead, Lydia, I'm fine here."

The two meticulously thorough shoppers finally approached the counter. If their debate was what they went through deciding what to buy in a tiny gift shop, he could only imagine what they must go through when facing a significant task. Marco had always prided himself on being a sociable person, but he wasn't feeling it at the moment. As the ladies approached the door on their way out, Marco opened it for them.

"Thank you," one said.

"You're so nice," the other said. "It's so rare to find manners like that anymore!"

Guilt overwhelmed him for a moment. The Gallery was, after all, a store. They had every right to shop there, regardless of Marco's personal problems. He turned back to Lydia, only to discover she'd escaped through the back door.

Allie glanced toward the back. "Better hurry."

Marco did just that. He caught up with her outside the back door. "Lydia, wait up!"

With her chin up, Lydia strode toward the street.

Marco ran to catch up. "Lydia, please, can we talk?"

"Why? So you can ruin my lunch?" She kept walking.

"I was hoping I might make it better."

A slight pink tinted her cheeks, which always

happened when she was angry. She had that porcelain skin characteristic of so many redheads, with a few tiny freckles that she tried to cover with makeup. He had seen her with and without her makeup. Either way, she looked pretty to him. It shouldn't have been, but the fire in her eyes at that moment was appealing, while her peach-colored lipstick made her lips look even fuller.

It can't be true, but it is. I've just lost a friend. Or maybe she has. It depends on which way you look at it. I can't believe this. Of course, she has no idea. Otherwise, while I had my traumatic revelation, she might have patiently waited—and possibly rendered aid. But no, she's walking briskly ahead with no interest in my agony.

He wasn't feeling too well. "Lydia, wait!"

Marco ran to catch up, then she stopped abruptly, causing him to nearly run into her. Thanks to four years on the basketball team, he had the agility to avoid a collision.

"Let me buy you lunch." He gave her his most smoldering look with a track record of making girls melt, but it got him nothing. *Dang. Twice in one day, the Silva charm failed.*

She stared over her red-rimmed glasses, which had an adorable habit of sliding down her nose. "How interesting that you think a free meal can buy my attention and your salvation."

"Oh, come on. I know I screwed up, but don't you think that's a little extreme?" He raised an eyebrow for further effect.

Lydia's lips started to curve upward.

Marco started to smile. "If I dig into my pocket change, I might be able to throw in some dessert."

MARCO WAS ACTING in a way that Lydia barely recognized. He wanted, perhaps even needed, her help. She'd always been the one who wanted more, although he never knew it. It felt good to be needed. At the same time, Lydia longed to be free.

Something was wrong with Marco. That much was obvious. He seemed to think she was the only one who could help him get through it. While the friend in her wanted to help him, the woman trying to get over him needed to leave him alone. Her ego had convinced her that he couldn't manage without her, but she knew that was false. He was an adult, and he would be fine.

Then there was Bryce. With Bryce, she felt normal again. They could go out and have a good time without her emotions tearing in different directions. She could spend an entire day with Bryce, feeling content and secure. He said and did all the right things until Lydia found herself imagining them going through life together in pleasant boredom. *Argh! But it's worse when your heart soars at the mere sight of someone who doesn't return the same feelings. Marco has ruined my heart, and he has no idea that every gesture of friendship is a stinging reminder of what I can't have. It's my own fault. Marco doesn't know, and he won't know because I won't tell him. It's time to grow up and stop doing this to myself.*

"Marco, I can't have lunch or dessert." He looked stunned, but he didn't protest, so Lydia went on. "There's a lot going on in my life right now. I promise it's nothing you did. I just need some time to myself. I could lie and say that I'm busy and not answer your calls, but I won't do that to you. Your friendship has meant a lot to me." He drew in a breath, but before he could speak, she interrupted. "It's a small town, so it's hard to avoid each other." She tried to smile, but it was hopeless. It was the wrong time for tears, so she fought them. "Let's just call it a breather." *That was the worst lie you've ever told in your life. This is goodbye forever.* Only Lydia's forever was worse, because Marco would always be in it, just out of reach.

LYDIA SKIPPED lunch and brought back a coffee.

Allie stuck her head in the doorway between the shop and the back room. "That was quick."

Barely nodding, Lydia sank into a chair facing the window. Crusted white snow coated the buildings and benches surrounding the harbor. A few forlorn fishing boats sat in the frozen water as if caught unaware of time passing around them. Winter could be so bleak, she thought.

Allie sat down next to Lydia, where she had a good view of the shop in case anyone wandered in. "What happened?"

As much as Lydia wished she could cry and just let it all out, she couldn't. All that misery lay locked in her heart with no hope of release. "I sort of broke up with Marco."

"Broke up? That sounds..."

"If it does, then it's my fault. We were just friends. I knew that. I guess I just reached a point where I couldn't be his friend anymore."

Allie said softly, "Because you feel more."

Lydia nodded as she stared at the horizon. "Bryce and I have been seeing each other. He likes me."

Allie's eyes brightened. "Well, that's good."

"It is." Lydia exhaled. "It's so much easier with

Bryce. Everything is calm and serene... and bland. But I think it could get better. Not everyone feels fireworks and heart-pounding longing. Love can take time to grow, right?"

Allie's eyebrows drew together. "I think so. It's different for everyone."

"I want it to be different for me." She took a sip of her coffee and savored its warmth and comforting flavor. "I think I hurt Marco's feelings."

"But he had to understand how you felt."

"He would have—if he knew."

"You didn't tell him?"

"I couldn't get the words out. I've already ripped open my heart. I couldn't just put it all out there for Marco to stomp all over."

"He cares too much about you to do that."

Lydia leaned back in her chair and stared up at the ceiling's edge with tear-moistened eyes. "I don't understand why, but having him care like that makes it worse, in a way. All that caring looks too much like what I wish I could be. It's like a carrot dangling in front of my face, and I'm the jackass."

Allie gently rubbed Lydia's shoulder then gave it a pat. "Don't you think you're being a little bit hard on yourself?"

"Yeah... I'm more of a cute little kitten in his eyes

—something to find adorable and play with for a while then set aside when something cuter comes along."

The bell over the shop door rang to announce customers. Allie said, "We'll talk later." She gave Lydia's hand a squeeze and went into the shop, gently closing the door behind her.

NINE

Marco returned to the brewpub in time to finish the lunch rush and do most of the side work.

Only then did Theo approach him. "Sit down."

Mel stopped by on her way out the door and leaned on the bar beside Marco. "You still owe me a full shift. That was the agreement."

He stared down at his hands. "Yeah, got it."

"Good, 'cause I'm going out for the evening, and my phone will be off."

Without looking at her, he said, "Good. Have fun."

Puzzled, she looked at Theo and exhaled loudly. "We could change it to tomorrow if you want."

Theo said, "That's okay. You go ahead."

"Are you sure?"

"Yeah, we're good. Thanks."

Theo slid onto the stool beside Marco. "So, what is it?"

Marco stared at the bottles lining the wall. "I'm not even sure what I did, but Lydia doesn't want to be friends anymore. I was a little irritable the other day, but she's got no right to complain about that. You should see her in the mornings."

"And you can't think of anything that might have prompted this?"

"No. I thought we were really good friends. That's how I felt, anyway. But she's just cut me off with no explanation."

"What about the new boyfriend?"

That touched a nerve. "Boyfriend? I wouldn't call him that."

"But maybe she would." Theo hastened to add, "I'm just guessing. But maybe her boyfriend—"

"Bryce." Marco smirked.

"Right. Maybe Bryce has something to do with this. I mean, it's kind of obvious, isn't it? He's probably jealous."

The thought bothered Marco. "That's a little possessive of him at this stage in the game, don't you think?"

Theo used his soothing parental tone, which at the moment irritated the heck out of Marco. "I don't know. Wouldn't you be? Look at it from his point of view. He's an outsider. He meets Lydia, and he's crazy about her. But she's got this guy in her life, and they're more than just friends."

"Hold on. No one said that."

Theo looked at him impatiently. "No one has to. He just has to see you two together."

"If that is, in fact, the problem, then Lydia solved it. She made her choice, and Bryce won."

Theo shook his head. "It shouldn't have to be a contest."

"Yeah? Tell that to Lydia."

"Give it time. It'll sort itself out."

Marco mulled it over, but it just didn't feel right. "Unless Bryce is some sort of control freak. That's what they do."

"You've lost me." Theo squinted in that parental way that he had when he wanted to be supportive but couldn't.

"I'm saying he could be one of those control freaks. One day they're dating, and the next day she's cut off ties to her family and friends, and he keeps her locked up at home and completely dependent on him."

Theo leaned back and studied Marco. "Do you really think that's what's going on? For one thing, Lydia would never put up with that."

"Good point, but still..."

"Marco, it's an interesting theory, but it's a little over the top."

"So if that's not the case, then she hates me."

Theo winced. "Well, you know what they say."

Marco rolled his eyes. "No, I don't."

Theo looked as though he was stating the obvious. "Occam's razor. The simplest explanation is usually the right one."

"Oh, great. Thanks."

Theo's eyes twinkled. "But in your case, it couldn't be that." He reached for Marco's chin, but Marco swatted him away. "Look at that face. What's not to love?"

"Me. Not that this has anything to do with love, because it doesn't. We're just talking hypotheticals, right?"

Marco looked too amused. "Oh, absolutely."

"But if she hates me, I can understand why. Look at me! Sitting here wringing my hands like a..."

"Person who wrings their hands a lot?" Theo laughed. "Look, why don't you go upstairs and take a little time for yourself. I'll be fine here—until dinner."

Marco thought for a moment then hopped off the stool. "I'm going out for a run."

Theo grabbed a rag and started to wipe down the counter, then he looked up and called to Marco, "It's the middle of December. Watch out for black ice!"

THE ROAD WAS CLEAR ENOUGH, but Marco was rusty. He'd been busy working and studying, and exercise had fallen by the wayside, and he was paying for it. But that was okay. It was time to begin a new phase in his life. Spending less time with Lydia would mean more time for running and schoolwork. Maybe that was all he needed—more running and fewer emotions.

His life had shifted so gradually that he never noticed it coming, but one day, he woke up to discover he was dependent upon Lydia. It began simply. They had fun being together, so he didn't think about how he looked forward to seeing her or how he missed her when something else got in the way. That was to be expected from friends who got along as well as they did, but they were always just that—friends. It wasn't as though they were dating. But a few months passed, and there she was—part of his life. He hadn't even seen it coming.

In a way, Lydia had done him a favor by severing ties. They'd become too close, and she must have known it. That was how people got hurt, although he always assumed that sort of pain was confined to a dating relationship, and emotional pain was what he sought to avoid above all.

When his mother had died, he was too young to know how to process his grief. Therapy helped him get through it. But the memory of that pain cemented his resolve to avoid feeling that way ever again. Since then, he had insulated himself from relationships that threatened to deepen.

It was never his aim to come across as a free-spirited guy who couldn't be pinned down, but once he realized that was how people perceived him, he went with it. It worked. Women in his life had low expectations, so no one got hurt. He liked it that way— or he used to. One thing he did not like was being rejected. The last person he would have expected it from was Lydia. She'd caught him off guard. Although quiet, she knew what she wanted—and it wasn't Marco. He inwardly groaned. It was Bryce.

※

As THE DAYS passed without seeing Marco, Lydia grew more accustomed to being without him. One evening, she sat beside Bryce as the curtain rose on a nearby college production of *The Nutcracker*. Marco would never have suggested it. She wasn't even sure if Marco owned a suit. Bryce did. In fact, he owned several. She knew that because they'd already attended a theatrical version of *A Christmas Carol* and two Christmas parties at the homes of family friends, and they had dined at a couple of really nice restaurants. Although he never spoke about it, it was apparent he had money. That was Bryce—humble, kind, and generous.

That wasn't to say Marco lacked any of those qualities. He might have lacked Bryce's wealth, but he was every bit as humble, kind, and generous as Bryce. Since she'd known Marco, he had been there for her when she needed it most. He'd been a really good friend. Since she'd ended the friendship, Lydia had repeated that thought process so many times. This was the part where the guilt settled in. Cutting Marco off with no real explanation must have hurt him. Looking back, she'd been selfish in her handling of it, but continuing on the path their relationship was on would have been too painful to bear.

Godfather Drosselmeyer's musical cue brought her back to the moment. Something had always been a little off about Drosselmeyer, but that was the beauty of Christmas. It cast a magical glow over even the most cringeworthy things—like having anyone, even a jolly red-suited man, able to see people when they're sleeping. That was such an unsettling thought. She supposed it was largely a matter of who was doing the seeing and when. For instance, she had no objection to

Marco climbing a tree and more or less flying through her window. It all depended on context.

Intermission came, and they sipped champagne while Bryce explained all about the family scrap-metal business, which was very successful, and Bryce would be the third generation to join it. Lydia admired them for having found something they all enjoyed doing. She hadn't even managed to declare a major, while Bryce had his whole life planned out for him. Knowing there would be no surprises or big decisions to make was appealing. His path was steady and secure. Yet as she thought about a life without surprises, she wondered if that was the right path for her.

Lydia forgot all thoughts of her future as the pas de deux enveloped her in its rapture. She had been trying to ignore it, but the resemblance between the wavy dark-haired Nutcracker and Marco was inescapable. That, combined with the beauty of her favorite scene of the ballet, brought her as close to a state of euphoria as anything in the world could. In that blissful moment, Bryce chose to pull out a cellophane-wrapped cough drop and begin to open it, crinkle by crinkle. Without thinking, Lydia reflexively reached over and clamped her hand over his, where she held it until the scene was over.

The audience was still applauding as the curtain

rose yet again for another well-deserved round of applause when Bryce got up and climbed over half a dozen laps until reaching the aisle, leaving Lydia to apologize her way down the row after him. As they stepped out into the street, it looked as though the same light snow from the first act was now drifting down to collect on their shoulders.

Bryce wasn't angry or even annoyed. In fact, he didn't seem to feel guilty at all. Nor did Lydia, because Bryce was the one in the wrong.

He sputtered a few words on their way to the car. "That was a little rude and uncalled for."

"So was unwrapping candy in the middle of the ballet. And not just any part of the ballet—the most glorious scene in the ballet. In *any* ballet. That pas de deux is the most stunningly uplifting—soaring—" She stopped.

He had the most curious look on his face, as though he were observing a new zoo exhibit. Then he surprised her. "I'm sorry. I had no idea it meant so much to you."

And to pretty much everyone sitting around us, but... whatever.

"Thank you for pointing that out. I won't do it again."

Lydia believed that he meant it. Even so, it was such an odd way to react. It was as though she had asked him to put the toilet seat down. What he'd done had affected other people. It was plainly inconsiderate for both the audience and the performers. But Bryce didn't care one way or the other except for the fact that it had bothered Lydia. And for her, he was willing to adjust his behavior. She wasn't quite sure how to take that. On the one hand, he was being considerate of her, but on the other hand, he was blissfully unaware of the people around him. In any event, the conflict was resolved.

For the rest of the evening, Lydia remained puzzled. They had weathered their first disagreement and come out unscathed. There was no drama, and that was a good thing. But no drama implied no emotion, and that troubled Lydia. With Marco, life was always dramatic but not in a negative way. They were the stars of their own ballet with no audience needed. Together, they plunged into each moment with laughter and zest. She couldn't recall a dull moment with Marco. On the other hand, Bryce cared for her in a dutiful way. With him, she knew just where she stood. That gave her a sense of safety and security that, at times, she had lacked in her life.

It was with some astonishment that Lydia realized she had what she'd always wanted. All her life, she had been different, the girl with no father and a mother with no financial security. She might have gone without nonessentials like skiing and shopping with friends at the mall, but she'd always had everything she needed. The fact that her mother had managed that much was astounding. Still, at the edge of their lives was the ever-present threat that they had no cushion if something went wrong. On any day, the threat loomed that they might not have enough. *Then where would we be?* Lydia never knew the answer. She only knew the subtle sense of dread underlying their lives.

Bryce had no worries. Everything seemed to fall into place whenever she was with him. Even the candy wrapper incident had faded away by the time he walked her to her door.

"You look pretty tonight." Then he kissed her—a light and chaste kiss, as always. "Good night." And he left.

He could have been kissing his elderly aunt, with the passion his kisses conveyed. He was a proper gentleman, which was fine—more than fine. Nothing was wrong with taking things slowly and methodically, except that Lydia felt like there ought to be more. The problem was that she didn't know. For that, she had only herself to blame. She had purposely avoided dating in high school, mainly because there hadn't been anyone she felt that way about. But she was suddenly in a position in which she lacked vital experience that might have given her a better frame of reference where men were concerned. For instance, she didn't mind kissing Bryce, but she couldn't help but wonder if that was all there was to it—because she didn't feel a thing.

Kissing and sex looked so great in the movies, but everything looked better on the screen. Real life couldn't be anything like that. Yet the big screen didn't come close to some aspects of real life. Nothing could compare to looking out from the harbor, not only to take in the changeable colors of the massive sea with its slow, powerful waves but also to be able to feel the sea air brush one's face and breathe in the salt-and-lobster-laced scent of the docks. It was an all-encompassing thrill to feel part of the power of nature. If real life could be so much better, kissing and sex ought to be too.

Lydia sighed. She was expecting too much.

This is where it would be helpful to have girlfriends to talk with about it. But that window had closed. No way could she, at the ripe age of eighteen, admit to having never experienced anything more than a chaste kiss. People would think she was a freak. She could only assume that was as good as it got until proven otherwise.

TEN

LYDIA WENT Christmas shopping for Bryce. Expectations were relatively low at that point in their relationship, but the choice still wasn't easy for her. Cologne seemed a little too personal, and the hats, gloves, and scarves didn't seem personal enough. Deciding felt like torture. She didn't know what Bryce would want, so she settled on something safe—a necktie.

As she stared at one, someone with a familiar voice said, "Bryce strikes me as more of a bowtie kind of guy."

She looked up to find Marco grinning at her. "I've never seen Bryce in a bowtie. Ever."

"He should really consider it. It would be a good look for him."

Lydia narrowed her eyes, but once she caught

sight of the mischievous light in Marco's, she couldn't help but smile.

"When you get down to my name on your list..." He leaned over her phone. "Just keep scrolling. It's way down there at the bottom."

She shoved her phone into her pocket.

Marco didn't even try to hide his amusement. "I'm not really a tie guy. Think rugged and manly." He picked up a Christmas tie with a large reindeer. "Something more like this. See, if you press it right here, his nose lights up."

"Oh, that's stunning."

"Right?" His grin faded, leaving a gentle smile. "And what about you?" He patted his thigh. "Come tell Santa what you'd like for Christmas."

You. I've missed you.

A wistful look settled on his face. She had forgotten how his gaze warmed her. Actually, she remembered but had tried to forget. Then every time he looked at her, it was like the first time.

She did her best to lighten the mood. "If Santa brought me a tie like that, I'd be the happiest girl in the world."

Marco made a poor attempt at a smile, which made it even harder for her to shrug off the charged silence that was settling between them.

At last, Marco asked, "How are you?"

"I'm sorry." She couldn't help blurting it. The apology had weighed upon her since she'd first caught sight of him. Not only had cutting things off so abruptly not helped her at all, but it had also hurt him.

Marco shook his head as though it were nothing, but the look in his eyes told a different story.

Lydia couldn't think of what else to say other than to tell him she hadn't wanted to see him because she cared for him too much. But she couldn't tell him that. Although if he didn't stop looking at her like that, she might lose her resolve.

A sales associate appeared out of nowhere. "May I help you?"

Startled, Lydia said, "Yes, would you ring this up, please?" She set down the tie she'd selected for Bryce then pulled out her debit card and handed it to the salesclerk.

Marco leaned his elbow on the counter. He was inches from her. It was all she could do to lift her eyes to meet his, knowing she might give away how being near him made her pulse race.

He said, "I miss having coffee."

"Have you given it up?" She was proud of herself for lightening the mood.

"With you. I miss having coffee with you."

So much for lightening the mood. Lydia reminded

herself that it was just coffee, yet she could barely string words together to speak. She managed a nod.

The sales associate handed her a stylish holiday handle bag. She thanked him then turned to Marco. *What now? "It was good seeing you? We'll have to do this again sometime?"*

"So... what I'm trying to ask is would you have coffee with me?"

"Now?" With the way her heart was pounding, anyone might've thought he had asked her for coffee and her hand in marriage. Saying yes felt as though she would be cheating on Bryce, which was ridiculous, but it was how she felt. Yet she said yes, surprising not only herself but, from the looks of him, Marco as well.

As they ordered their coffee, they were light and chatty like they'd always been together, but an undercurrent of tension ran through the conversation. A crowd filled the coffee shop, but a Christmas miracle brought them to a table just as a couple was leaving. They plopped down victoriously and exhaled. After their first sips, the mood took a turn.

The usually good-humored Marco sometimes turned into the other Marco, which even Lydia only glimpsed rarely. His eyes darkened. "I'm sorry."

"For what?" Their parting had been Lydia's decision.

"For being apart. For whatever I did to cause it."

He looked down and played with a corner of his napkin.

"You didn't do anything." Her face flushed. "Life got a little confusing. I needed some time to myself."

"And now?"

Lydia had never seen Marco look so vulnerable. "Now? I..." *Don't know what to say. Yes, I want to spend time with you—all the time—because I'm in... trouble. The L-word I can't let myself say kind of trouble.*

"Are we... okay?"

Something inside Lydia's brain clicked into emergency backup mode. Her face artificially brightened. "Yes! Absolutely! Like I said, you didn't do anything wrong. I had some things to sort out in my life, and I've sorted them out. Everything's good. I've touched base with my father, and we're building something. Bryce and I couldn't be better. And you and I are good friends—just like always."

Marco nodded as though he wanted to believe her, but doubt lingered in his eyes. "Good. Well, that's great." Then Marco turned back into his old self again and grinned. "So if I see you around, you won't be firing candy canes at me with a crossbow?"

"Well, I can't lie. That does sound like fun, but I think we'll be fine." *Which is why I want to get up and run to my car and bury my face in my hands—because that's what I do over all my best friends.* Lydia couldn't hold her fake smile for much longer, so she said, "It was great seeing you, but I've got to get going. Say hi to Theo."

"I will." He made no move to leave.

"Bye, Marco." She picked up her shopping bags and walked away, stunned.

Who am I kidding? I love him.

Lʏᴅɪᴀ sᴀɴᴋ into her car seat and locked the door. *What have I done?* She'd always found Marco attractive, and nothing was wrong with a little crush. But the crush kept getting deeper. Though she had convinced herself the feelings would pass, they hadn't.

They had blossomed into love. She didn't know when it had happened or even what made her so sure it was love. As many poems as she'd read or love songs she'd heard, no one had ever managed to define love to her satisfaction. Yet she had never been surer of anything in her life. Maybe their separation had cleared her head, but it hadn't done much for her heart. As she'd sat there with Marco, fresh emotions overwhelmed her. Like a tidal current, she couldn't see it or hold it in her hands, but it swept her away with its power. Even if her emotion wasn't love, it felt totally unlike what she felt for Bryce.

Lydia hit the steering wheel. "I am not going to let one random encounter with Marco ruin my one chance at happiness. Bryce likes me, and our relationship is going somewhere. I may not know where that is, but I know it won't hurt like this."

ELEVEN

ONE OF THE many remarkable things about Caroline Welch was that she knew how to throw a good party. The evening began with valet parking. Bryce handed over the keys.

"Wait! I almost forgot the Secret Santa present."

Lydia started for the car, but Bryce stopped her and retrieved it himself. Then they went into the house. Lydia had been there before, but Caroline's house had transformed to look even more like a magazine layout with fresh, fragrant evergreen and holly decorations. Poinsettias adorned the massive food buffet, while mistletoe hung in well-chosen locations.

Lydia wore a vintage deep-red velvet dress she'd found in a resale shop, while Bryce wore a black suit and a green-and-navy-striped tie. The house was brimming with people Lydia didn't know, most of whom she presumed were Caroline's clients and business acquaintances. While she glanced about, hoping to find someone she recognized, Bryce took two glasses of champagne from a passing server. They stood sipping champagne and talking. Christmas couldn't get much more festive.

Almost a week had gone by since Lydia's chance coffee meeting with Marco, and she'd decided it was time to face up to the truth. She genuinely felt for and probably loved him. They would always be friends on some level, but Lydia needed to think of herself. Loving someone who didn't love you back was not a long-term prescription for happiness. Lydia couldn't blame Marco. She doubted he knew. But every kindness he bestowed upon her broke her heart.

With that knowledge, she could take positive action by being good to herself and doing what was emotionally healthy for her. She was going to put distance between them but more subtly than last time. Her attempt at a clean break had been too drastic and impossible to sustain. She would make no grand statement but see him less frequently until she'd successfully moved on with her life. This time, she meant it.

Theo and Allie arrived, much to Lydia's delight.

Allie was one of her favorite people to talk to. *This is going to be fun.*

Then she saw Marco. He walked in wearing a sports coat and a red cashmere sweater. That was as dressed up as she'd ever seen him—and as handsome. Only a strikingly virile man could pull off the anti-suit look. But when he could accomplish it, women took notice. Lydia certainly did. *Why does he have to keep doing that?* Some things just weren't fair.

As she observed Marco, Bryce struck up a conversation with a couple nearby. He introduced Lydia as his girlfriend, which was a first. She supposed she was. They had just never put it into words. It had a nice sound that she didn't mind at all. It hinted at a future together, which was what she hoped for with Bryce.

Bryce's new friends were describing a cruise they'd just taken. As nice as it sounded, detailed accounts of couples' vacations never interested others as much as they did them. Without meaning to, Lydia let her eyes wander. Marco was schmoozing as only he could. It was a gift. The guy had never met a stranger.

Allie waved to Lydia. She whispered something to Theo then crossed the room to join Lydia. They raved about each other's frocks, and Allie looked gorgeous in royal-blue satin.

"Wouldn't you love to be Caroline for a day?" Allie asked.

Lydia laughed. "This is pretty amazing."

Allie's friend Kim joined them. "Too bad she's too nice for us to resent her for it."

Allie said, "I know. But she is. So you've just got to love her."

Theo put his arm around Allie's shoulder. "Miss me?"

Slipping her arm around his back, she said, "Desperately."

Lydia turned to Bryce to draw him into the conversation, but he was involved in a deep discussion of cruise lines, so she turned back to Allie. As she did, a familiar voice made her heart skip a beat.

"Who's your friend, Allie?" Then Marco appeared at her side. He turned to Lydia and said, "Wow."

Lydia's eyebrows drew together. "Thank you?"

He looked almost too amazed, making her wonder how she must look the rest of the time.

"You look so... pretty."

If he didn't stop looking at her like that, Lydia might swoon. So far, her plan of putting distance between them wasn't going too well, but Christmas was always different. It involved new rules for eating and drinking and talking to guys you were in love with. She was losing her heart, and more than a New Year's resolution was required to remedy the situation.

She needed to get back to the friend zone. Smiling, she said, "I'm surprised you're not here with a date."

Though she'd expected a clever quip, he just gave her a puzzled expression. "When's the last time you saw me with a date?"

"I don't know. I guess I haven't—not in a while." Lydia felt so uncomfortable that she wanted to flee. Drawn into his brooding gaze, she fought back with a laugh. "Given how you feed on attention from women, you must be starving."

Her attempt at humor fell flat. He muttered, "Don't believe everything you hear."

With his usual perfect timing, Bryce turned and put his arm around Lydia's waist. "Oh, hi, Marco."

They shook hands, then Marco said, "Speaking of starving, I'm going to check out the buffet." Then he left.

Lydia's mom and Dylan joined Bryce and Lydia for a quick hello on their way to see Caroline. Kim flitted over to chat then left just as quickly. Lydia felt as though everything was going on all around her like a carousel, and she stood alone in its midst yet somehow apart.

Her face felt hot. Before she embarrassed herself

by turning into a freckly beet, she said, "Excuse me," and headed down the hall.

The only place where she might have a moment alone was the bathroom, but that was already occupied. Lydia headed upstairs to the master bath. Having been in Caroline's house before, she knew where everything was. Once there, she filled her hands with cold water then lifted them to her face. At the last second, she remembered she was wearing makeup and velvet, neither of which would look good splashed with water. So she moistened one of Caroline's guest towels and blotted her cheeks.

Just get through Christmas. You can do this. So what if there are tons of parties and events that you'll both be attending? The holiday will fly by, then you'll have the freezing-cold winter to hibernate indoors. Months will pass. We'll barely see each other.

Lydia looked herself up and down in the mirror then smoothed her dress. *Look at you looking... pretty. See? Everything's fine.*

She pulled open the door, and Marco stood inches from her. "Oh, sorry! Excuse me." She tried to sidle around him to get a clean shot at the stairs.

He held her shoulders. "Hey, wait. Is everything okay?"

She drew in a breath. "Sure. Why wouldn't it be?"

He lowered himself to her eye level. "Because I know you."

"Not everything about me." But he knew all the relevant stuff, so she couldn't meet his eyes.

"I know that the edges of your ears get a little bit red when you're stressed or upset. Something's wrong."

"Well, isn't that just like a man?" *What do I even mean by that?* He was probably wondering that, too, and he would ask her if she didn't distract him. She lifted her chin. "If you must know, I had to go to the bathroom. It happens."

She tried so hard to look slightly perturbed yet unruffled, but he didn't buy her act for a minute.

With a smirk, he said, "I thought all women powdered their noses in pairs. Isn't that what they do in the movies?"

"Not any movie since 1950." She tried to look over his shoulder to the stairs, which was ridiculous considering their heights. "So now that we've had our little film retrospective, would you mind if I went back downstairs?"

Marco looked lost, which completely threw Lydia. She wasn't even sure what to call it. Every bit of his usual bravado was gone.

He asked, "What are you doing?"

He looked too intense to be kidding, so she

resisted the urge to say something snarky. "I don't know what you mean."

"What are you doing with him?"

"Who? Bryce?"

Anger flared in his eyes. "Of course Bryce—unless there's someone else you're wasting your time with."

"Since when do you care how I waste—spend my time?"

"Since I've known you."

Lydia wanted to say so many things, but she refused to.

"Dammit, Lydia, we're friends—better than friends. You can't expect me to just stand here and watch this train wreck without doing something!"

"Train wreck? Oh, wow. I am so lucky to have someone like you to rescue me. For the first time in my life, I've found someone who cares about me."

"I care!"

"Not like that. Bryce cares about me. And I'm happy, so leave me alone."

She pushed past him. At the same time, he took a step back, throwing Lydia off balance. Marco took her arm long enough to steady her then stepped aside and let go.

Once downstairs, she headed for the kitchen, forgetting that the catering crew would be all over it. Then she stepped outside the back door. It was well below freezing, but at least her face didn't feel hot anymore. She stood on the deck for a moment. The distant harbor lights were blurry in the night sky.

Sometimes it seemed as though Marco was deliberately torturing her with his version of friendship. He couldn't know what he did to her. Every time he told her he cared, it came with an unspoken reminder that he didn't care enough. Lydia shivered and went back inside. She only hoped she didn't see Marco again, though she couldn't avoid him completely unless she asked Bryce to take her home early. But she would need a reason. Complaining of a headache would work. Then she would be free of Marco, at least for the night.

"There you are!" Bryce exclaimed as he put an arm around her shoulders and drew her against him.

Of course, Marco was standing nearby with Theo and Allie. She caught Allie's eye and her concerned expression, but Lydia averted her eyes as though nothing were wrong. Caroline announced it was time for the gift exchange. Those who had chosen to participate were to gather around the Christmas tree.

"Bryce, I've got a headache. Would you mind taking me home?"

With appropriate sympathy, he stroked her cheek and said, "Oh, sure. Right after this."

"But—"

Bryce turned, and Lydia gave up. She could endure one little gift exchange, so she braced herself and went along it. Lydia had drawn Theo's name. She'd consulted with Allie and chosen a travel kit of his favorite cologne. He seemed happy with it, which gave her a few moments' distraction. While others took their turns opening gifts, Lydia rehearsed her exit strategy. Then Lydia's turn came. She opened her gift to find a man's necktie—a blinking reindeer tie like the one Marco had shown her in the store.

See, if you press it right here, his nose lights up. She remembered his words and touched the button so lightly that nothing happened.

At a complete loss for words, Lydia looked at him.

"Here, I'll show you how it works." Marco squatted by her chair and lifted the tie.

Something fell from it and landed inside the box. Clasped together was a pair of pearl earrings that had been unceremoniously tucked inside the folds of the tie. Lydia lifted her eyes.

Marco answered her unspoken question with a nod and said softly, "They're real."

"But—" They were clearly outside of the gift-exchange limit.

"No buts. You can't argue with Santa."

They moved on to the next gift as Marco said,

"Merry Christmas," then left before she could wish him the same.

After the gift exchange, Lydia said she was hungry and escaped to the buffet in the next room. She wasn't, but she needed a few moments to think, then she returned to Bryce.

"Lydia, I was just telling Theo and Allie about my family's holiday bash. They throw it every year for the company and their friends. It's a pretty big event that people look forward to."

"Sounds fantastic." It didn't at the moment, but she was being polite. Right then, her idea of a fantastic evening would be sitting at home by the fire with a book that would take her away.

Bryce grinned and pulled an envelope from his inside jacket pocket, and Marco chose that moment to reappear at Theo's side.

Handing the envelope to Lydia, Bryce said, "Merry Christmas."

They hadn't planned to exchange gifts that evening. It hardly seemed appropriate in the middle of someone else's party, and they suddenly had a small audience.

"Go on. Open it."

"Here?"

"Sure."

Lydia wasn't sure she was ready for another surprise, but she opened the envelope.

"It's a train ticket," Bryce said. He was always so helpful. He looked so happy that Lydia made an effort to smile, but it didn't reach her eyes.

He said, "It's for next weekend—so you can come to my family's holiday party. I have to go home tomorrow, and with the nor'easter coming next weekend, I didn't want you to drive. I thought you could come on the train. You can stay for the weekend. Don't worry. We've got a huge house— plenty of room. It's all settled."

All settled? "We're pretty busy at work."

"Allie just told me she could spare you."

Lydia turned to Allie, who smiled, probably convincingly for anyone else, but Lydia knew better. Allie had to have thought she was doing Lydia a favor, and she couldn't make Allie change her mind. Lydia felt Marco's eyes on her. She would not give him the satisfaction of thinking she was anything but delighted, so she turned to Bryce and thanked him warmly.

Bryce gave her shoulder a squeeze. "You don't know what a good time you're in for. I can't believe I didn't think of this sooner."

It was such a nice gesture that Lydia wanted to be happy about it. Besides, his taking her home to meet his parents was a sign their relationship was headed in a positive direction. She and Bryce were building something together that would get her mind off Marco. When she looked at it like that, she began to feel hope. Maybe the weekend would be just what she needed.

TWELVE

Bryce was in his element, talking golf and the market with likeminded people who spoke the same language. Lydia had been deluding herself. They weren't going anywhere soon, so Lydia seized the moment to fade away and find a quiet corner for some alone time. She decided that Caroline's workout room would be perfect. No one would think to go there. She sat at a bench by the wall of windows, which were dark except for the Pine Harbor lights in the distance. She pulled Marco's earrings from her pocket. They were perfect in the worst sort of way. Kindness and generosity would only go to her head—or her heart. A sudden yearning overtook her to wear them, so she put them on.

She'd been there all of a minute when Marco

slipped inside and closed the door. It couldn't have happened by chance. He had followed her.

Her heart pounded at the sight of him. *Why does it always have to do that?* "Thank you for the earrings. They're beautiful."

He walked over and sat beside her. "They'll be beautiful on you."

Please don't say things like that—unless you want to break my heart. Never mind. It's too late for that.

He studied her for a moment then brushed her hair back. He looked pleased. "You're wearing them."

She didn't want to smile, but he always managed to coax one out of her. She shrugged. "I didn't want to lose them."

He kept his hand on her neck, with his thumb touching her earlobe. Lydia fought to remain still and not lean into his hand like a kitten.

"I didn't want to leave things the way we left them."

"We're okay, Marco."

He smiled gently. "But it's Christmas. We should be better than okay."

Lydia looked into the darkness beyond the window. *Do not let that tear drop.* She lifted her hand to her face and tried to wipe her emotions away.

"Hey," Marco whispered. He touched her chin and guided her face back toward his. "What's the matter?" A flash of anger burned in his eyes. "Has Bryce said something? That tool."

He started to stand, but Lydia caught him by the sleeve.

"No! He's the only thing good in my life!"

Marco's jaw dropped. "Really? You hide it so well."

"I don't know what you mean."

He looked away with a cynical smile. "Let's just say you're both very formal."

"Formal?"

"Distant? Cold?"

If his last remark had left her feeling defensive, that one finished the job. "We're not distant or cold. We're just different. Just because we don't paw each other in public doesn't mean that we're formal."

"Oh, so you paw each other in private."

"No! You're twisting my words."

Marco folded his arms. "Well then, explain it in your words."

She didn't like where the conversation was going, but she needed to set the record straight. "Real life is not like the movies. They make it seem like it's all fireworks and..."

"Romance?" His gaze bored through her facade.

Unable to bear his knowing look, Lydia protested.

"We don't need romance because we have something... real!"

Marco lifted his eyebrows and acted impressed, but she saw the sarcasm beneath it. "I see."

"Good." Her temper was not helping her case, so she tried to calm down.

"And I'm sorry." That time, he was being sincere, but the pity in his eyes stung far worse than his sarcasm.

"Why would you say that?"

His eyes had a faraway look. "I am the last one to give advice about love, but I think there's a lot to be said for a good fireworks display. I want more than that." He added, "For you... with Bryce."

Sometimes we don't have a choice. "What makes you think you can counsel me about love when you've never had a relationship that lasted more than a week?"

"That's not true! I've had a couple that lasted a month."

"I stand corrected. You're a love expert—as well as a commitment-phobe."

A hard look came into his eyes. "Love hurts, so I'm cautious. But it's not that I don't want to love or be loved. I just have to be sure."

"No one's ever sure."

"Maybe it's a matter of trust. Whatever it is, you're

wrong. I've always wanted to feel that kind of love, but I've just never found it." His searching eyes were so penetrating that Lydia feared he might find something she wasn't ready to share. She looked away.

Marco said, "You were about to tell me that something was wrong."

"Was I?" *I don't think so.*

"Is it your father?"

Lydia shook her head.

"Your mom? Dylan?"

"Marco, I'm fine. It's okay."

"Are you sure?"

"Yes!" She smiled and thought it had been fairly convincing.

"But?"

Lydia shook her head again. "But what? Maybe you're the one with the problem. In which case, don't look at me. I can't figure you out."

"I'm a pretty simple guy."

Lydia laughed. "You are anything but that. You are the most complicated person I've ever met." She considered her words, not wanting to reveal too much of the truth. "I don't understand why it's gotten so hard for us to be friends. It used to be so easy."

"Maybe we care too much."

Definitely on my part. "I used to think you

couldn't care too much because caring's a positive thing."

He smiled. "That's what I love about you. You see things so simply."

"And that's what I hate about you. You've always underestimated me."

He touched her cheek as he searched her eyes. "Not always. Not now."

If she didn't look away, she would drown in a sea of emotion. "Bryce will be wondering where I am."

Marco lifted his eyebrows. It was almost dismissive, but she couldn't be sure. She needed to go, and if finding Bryce served as her excuse, then so be it. She donned a bright smile. "Hey, it's Christmas! Look at us. We're at an amazing party! Let's not waste it in Caroline's exercise room."

"It's not wasted if I'm with you."

Oh, you're good. Really good. You should stop now. If you won't, I'll have to. But she didn't.

Marco's smile faded, and a look of surprise crossed his face. He gazed so deeply into Lydia's eyes that she felt a little lightheaded. His lips parted, and she parted hers. Then he touched his lips to hers gently. His were soft, and their mouths fit together. If she had looked down to discover she was floating, she wouldn't have been surprised.

Slowly, he pulled away and stared at her. She

didn't understand why he looked so confused when, for once, she was not. Everything felt right to her.

"If Bryce is the one, then I wish you the best. Merry Christmas." He kissed her on the forehead and left, closing the door gently behind him.

A tear trailed down Lydia's cheek as she whispered, "Merry Christmas."

In no hurry to return to the party, Lydia waited until she felt fully composed. She was getting better at it. Getting over Marco's gestures of friendship had become almost a routine. That kiss was a new addition, though, as cruel as it was tender. She wasn't sure she would ever understand what had just happened, so she shelved it along with her aching emotions. Though she could pull it off the shelf now and then to relive it. That kiss had enough in it to relive for the rest of her life.

Lydia sighed. She would be sighing a lot when she thought about Marco. But she couldn't build a life on a knee-buckling kiss from a friend. So Lydia drew in a deep breath, exhaled, and went upstairs to face real life.

"THERE SHE IS."

Bryce took Lydia's hand. He seemed happy to see

her, and she felt the same—or maybe she felt relieved. Bryce was fresh air to her lungs after the weight of confusion and heartache of being with Marco.

"I just spoke to your mother." He grinned at Eve. "And I've assured her that my parents will chaperone us." He leaned toward Eve and Dylan in mock confidence. "I've heard rumors that my mother has personally refocused the interior security cameras, so I assure you, your daughter will be well looked after." He put his arm around Lydia's shoulders.

Lydia marveled at how easily her mother had granted her approval for the trip. She had to have been as shocked by the invitation as Lydia was. While Lydia was old enough to make her own decisions, she and her mother were close. She respected Eve too much to go against her advice on such a trip. But her mother approved. That alone had to be some sort of sign that her relationship with Bryce was meant to be.

Lydia hadn't noticed Kim standing nearby until she pointed over Lydia's head. "Ahem! Mistletoe alert!"

Lydia looked up and tried not to wince. She still tasted Marco's kiss on her lips, but all eyes were on them.

Bryce looked delighted as he slid his arm down to her waist and dipped her for a dramatic kiss. It must have looked tremendously romantic, but she felt nothing. It was pleasant enough, but one kiss with Marco had convinced her she could have more. Nevertheless, the applause said everyone else had enjoyed it—all but one.

As Bryce returned her to a standing position, Lydia caught a glimpse of Marco's clouded expression as he leaned, arms folded, against the opposite wall. It would have been so much easier if he'd done what anyone else would have done, which was look away and pretend their eyes had never met. But he looked straight at her, almost glaring, and she felt that old weightlessness in her chest. Her confusion came back.

Lydia looked away, but she couldn't pretend that their eyes hadn't met—or their lips.

THIRTEEN

Lydia filled her work schedule for the week to make up for the time she would be away at Bryce's party. Allie assured her she didn't have to, but it was better than having too much time to think. Customers flocked to the shop during the holidays, so she managed to keep her thoughts from straying to Marco.

She and her father had gotten together a couple of times. Lydia was still getting used to discovering him at that point in her life, but Jack was making an effort, and they were building a relationship. She'd feared that he might want nothing to do with her, but that didn't happen. Lydia's mother didn't fully trust him yet, but he'd been good to Lydia, so that was a start. Jack and Lydia had made plans to get together before Christmas. He'd even invited her to his house on Christmas Day, for which she was thankful but had graciously declined. Her mother had Dylan, but Lydia couldn't imagine Christmas without her, so home was where she would be.

With only a few days left before Christmas, Lydia left work early and met Jack halfway between their homes for a pre-Christmas lunch. Lydia gave him a classic car ornament, and Jack gave her a pearl necklace.

It was a generous gift, but Jack dismissed the expense. "Every woman needs a pearl necklace."

"This must be my Christmas for pearls. A friend of mine gave me a pair of pearl earrings. They'll look perfect together."

Jack studied her with a twinkle in his eye. "Pearl earrings? Nice friend."

"He is."

Jack grinned. "Judging by the look in your eyes, I think he must be pretty special."

He had caught her off guard, and she couldn't cover what she suspected was written all over her face. Lydia had never been a good liar, and she didn't want to start with her father. "He's special to me."

"But?"

"But... I'm not sure I'm so special to him."

Jack leaned back. "Those earrings look pretty special. Hey, wait a minute. Is this the guy you told me about? The one who owns the restaurant?"

She nodded reluctantly.

"And the one who came to my car dealership with you."

"Yes, that was Marco." She hadn't meant to talk so much about him, but his name just came up in conversation. Though she tried to fight it, she'd always had an uncontrollable tendency to say what was on her mind. Most of the time, that was Marco. It didn't matter what she said. The truth came out as clearly as if she were holding a placard. She muttered, "I guess I've mentioned him one or two too many times."

Jack had the most wistful look on his face, almost as though he were saddened by something she hadn't told him. Maybe her tendency for punishing herself was a genetic predisposition that he saw in her and instinctively understood. Or perhaps he had something in his eye. Lydia still couldn't get a complete read on him. Her mother and Dylan had given her the impression that Jack was an insensitive jerk, and her mother had good cause to hold that opinion. But Lydia saw a different Jack and wondered if life hadn't changed him for the better in the years since high school. She often saw sad wisdom in his eyes.

Jack said, "A man who gives a woman pearl earrings has some pretty definite feelings for her."

Lydia couldn't believe she was talking about it, but

he was the one who had brought Marco's name up. Maybe her father could understand it from a man's point of view. *What harm could it do to discuss it with him?* "I think he does have definite feelings. Unfortunately, they're different from mine."

That seemed to make Jack angry. "Is he taking advantage of you?"

"No! Not the way that you're thinking. It's more like he wants my friendship. I don't think he realizes how hard it is for me to be with him. I've tried to put distance between us, but he just won't let go."

"And you haven't told him how you feel."

"No, and I won't."

Jack scratched his head then smoothed back his hair. "God knows I've screwed up my own life pretty royally over the years, but one thing I've learned is to be honest with people. If you can't be honest with Marco, maybe he needs to be honest with you."

"Or maybe it's not meant to be."

Jack leaned forward. "Well, if he ever hurts you, you just let me know."

Lydia couldn't help but smile. She'd never had a father to stand up for her. It was sweet, and it made her feel cared for. "Thanks, Jack. That means a lot."

As Lydia drove home, Bryce called, and they talked about the upcoming party. It sounded like fun. It was a big company party that filled their whole house. She was beginning to realize what a large house it must be. They would have musicians and a full staff on board to attend to everyone's needs. She'd glimpsed that world from afar, but Bryce offered a closer look. If things worked out between them, that world could be hers. She had never dreamed of wealth or glamour—although she wouldn't mind season tickets to the ballet and the opera—and when she was with Bryce, it almost felt like she was living someone else's life. Still, it was a good life, and she would enjoy it because Bryce was there with her.

Every evening at the brewpub had been busy lately, especially during the Christmas season, when so many were off for the holidays. Marco poured himself into the spirit of things, chatting up guests at the bar and trying to forget about Lydia. The thought of her trip to Bryce's house had been nagging at him all week. The closer it got to her trip, the more Marco fought to forget it. But the next day would come, and Lydia would go. Life could be cruel like that.

Too late, he'd discovered he liked Lydia as more

than a friend. Poor fool that he was, he loved her. Although it was his first time falling in love, his failure at it was in keeping with his track record with women. He sometimes thought he might tell Lydia his feelings were changing. While he was able to admit to himself how he felt, conveying his feelings to her was another story. He occasionally suspected that she felt the same, but then she pulled back and put distance between them. Marco hadn't planned to kiss Lydia. He'd tried to tell her how he felt. The kiss should have gotten her attention, at least. But even then, her thoughts were on Bryce. She was determined to get back to him, so Marco let her go.

Caroline's party had sealed the deal. When Bryce handed her a ticket to his version of paradise, Lydia was his. It didn't matter whether Marco thought she was making a mistake or that he didn't like Bryce. Lydia did like him, and that was all that mattered. Bryce had won. She would meet Bryce's family, which would level up their relationship significantly. In the end, Lydia made her choice. *But oh, what a waste of a kiss.* No one could convince him that she kissed Bryce like that. In fact, he'd had the misfortune to see them kiss. They had no passion between them, but that didn't matter because they were together, passion or not.

Marco grabbed a rag and wiped down the bar,

which was already clean. No matter how much he tried to rationalize things, in the back of his mind, a nagging suspicion that Lydia returned his feelings on some level persisted. That made it hard to let go and even harder to watch her in someone else's arms. But real love was unselfish, which meant he would step back from Lydia's life and watch her find happiness with Bryce Rumsey.

At least real love didn't mean that he had to like Bryce. No love was that strong.

FOURTEEN

THE DAY CAME for Lydia's trip to Bryce's home, and Marco was determined to ignore it. He worked long hours and entertained patrons with a frenetic energy that left people laughing and shaking their heads. But no matter how busy he was mixing drinks or pulling drafts, he couldn't drive Lydia out of his mind. It was so bad that when Lydia's father walked into the brewpub, Marco thought he was hallucinating. He had only seen him once on his way up in a balloon, but the resemblance was uncanny. When the man sat down at the bar, Marco was certain he had to be Lydia's father.

"Jack?"

The man nodded.

Marco was not going mad. That much was a relief.

So he extended his hand and introduced himself. "I'm a friend of your daughter's—of Lydia's."

Jack smiled and nodded amiably again.

"What can I get you?"

"Club soda."

When a guy drove an hour away for a drink, he usually had a good reason. He almost always had a reason for ordering a club soda too. So Lydia's father must be sitting before him for a specific reason. It didn't take a genius to figure out it had something to do with Lydia.

Marco got straight to the point. "How's Lydia?"

"Don't you know?"

Marco assumed his full bartender persona, smiling and chatting while he washed glasses and hung them on a rack overhead. "Well, we've been kind of busy here."

"Yeah, so I hear." He said it in a pointed way that got Marco's attention.

"So I haven't seen her in a few days. Is there something I should know about?"

Jack tilted his head. "That's why I'm here—to find out."

Marco had the uncanny sensation he was about to be pummeled, but he wasn't sure why.

Jack studied Marco with narrowing eyes. "You remind me a lot of myself when I was your age."

Given what Lydia had told him about her father's youth, Marco couldn't construe that as a compliment. Moreover, Jack's pumpkin festival had all the earmarks of a man who was all show and no substance. *So what have I done to give anyone a similar impression?* Then Lydia's words echoed in his head. She had as much as accused him of being like her father when she said he'd never managed to have a long-term relationship. Until that moment, he hadn't seen a connection to Jack, but it was obvious. Marco couldn't deny that he wasn't one to commit. Guys like that were out for short-term fun but lacked the depth of character to sustain a relationship. That was the man people assumed him to be. But Marco only cared about what Lydia thought.

For a man in his midthirties at most, Jack's sage—if not superior—attitude seemed undeserved, uncalled for, and not to mention irritating. It reminded Marco of when Theo had first become his guardian. It was hard to take orders from someone who, until recently, had been his equal, a brother who was only a few years older than he. But because Jack was Lydia's father, Marco would listen politely to what he had to say.

Jack said, "I've made some mistakes, and it took me a while, but I've learned from them. One of the things I learned was to make amends with the people

I've hurt. I should've done it with Eve, but at least this is a start. I intend to make up for lost time and look out for Lydia."

Marco listened, hoping he looked like he understood. The truth was that Jack had lost him. It almost seemed as though he was implying that Lydia needed protection from Marco. That really grated on him, since he'd been the one who was there for Lydia before she ever knew she had a father, so Jack could sit on his sanctimonious attitude.

Jack went on, "It's important to me to make up for the damage I've done by neglecting her all these years. She needed a father, and I failed her."

No one's arguing that point. For Lydia's sake, Marco was civil. "I know it's meant a lot to her to reconnect with you. For what it's worth, she's overcome any difficulties she might have had in the past. Your daughter is pretty amazing."

"I'm glad to hear that you've noticed."

That had a decidedly negative tone, but he couldn't quite pinpoint Jack's angle. "Of course I've noticed. We're friends—more than friends. I care a lot about Lydia."

In the silence that followed, which drew out until it became awkward, Marco could almost hear him thinking.

No longer able to endure the tension, Marco

asked, "Is something the matter? What are you trying to tell me? Is Lydia sick? Is there something that she hasn't told me?" The more he tried to guess what it might be, the more worried he got. People sometimes withheld vital information, often about health, in the false hope of sparing others. Lydia might have forbidden Jack from telling Marco, and Jack was trying to tell him without betraying his daughter's trust. "Look, if Lydia's sick, you have to tell me! I don't care if she told you not to say anything! I need to know!" He started untying his apron as he called Mel over. "Something's happened to Lydia. I need you to cover the bar."

Puzzled, Mel said, "Okay."

Marco turned back to Jack. "Tell me everything. Where is she? What can I do?"

Jack's eyes shone with pleasure. "Lydia isn't sick."

"Thank god!"

"Unless you count love. She's in love, and the person she's in love with is breaking her heart."

"I'll kill him."

Apparently amused, Jack said, "Well, you could, but that would just make things worse."

"I don't care. Give me Bryce's address, and I'll take care of him." Marco paused and took a breath. "I didn't mean that I'll literally kill him. It's just an expression—not that the thought doesn't have its appeal." What Marco hadn't ruled out was a punch in the face—maybe two. That was entirely doable.

"Bryce?" Jack laughed. "Bryce has nothing to do with this. You are so much like I was that it's scary, because you're a damn fool. No, genius, it's not Bryce she's in love with. It's you." Jack shook his head, threw a twenty on the bar, and walked out.

Snow flew at the windshield as Lydia drove to the train station. *This is a huge turning point for me.* By making the adult decision to build the life she wanted to lead, she was free of Marco and the baggage of the past. At the center of that life was Bryce. Of course, they hadn't made any sort of long-term commitment, but meeting the family was a pretty big step. *Who knows what the next year could bring?*

She imagined what life with Bryce could be. His career path was set. He would go into the family business, and she would fall into step with the rest of the family. Lydia imagined that, like Bryce, they were pleasant, cultured, and well-dressed, if not well-read. Bryce wasn't exactly a reader, but Lydia read enough for both of them. She envisioned their evenings together, Lydia in a comfy chair in the corner, reading a book while Bryce watched TV. He had his favorite sports teams and sitcoms, which he often spoke of. Though she thought they were funny, she found other things more entertaining.

Sitting at the bar, watching Marco at work, was always entertaining. The way he juggled drink mixing and joking with customers up and down the full length of the bar was like a ballet. What none of them saw was the real Marco, which she was privileged to know. Yet she had accused him of being shallow—and a commitment-phobe. The thought made her wince. She'd only said it because it would hurt him, but pride kept her from retracting her words. Lydia had seen glimpses of depth in Marco that almost overwhelmed her. He felt things deeply, he was kind and dependable, and he'd always been there for her. Not having met the right woman didn't make him a commitment-phobe any more than her not having found the right man did. Marco would meet the right woman just as she had found Bryce—not that Bryce was perfect, but he was a good man.

With all the confusion between Marco and her resolved, the pathway was clear for him. Then everyone would be happy.

But Lydia's memory was a problem. She couldn't seem to forget him, as hard as she tried. And the more she tried to force Bryce onto the pedestal vacated by Marco, the worse Bryce appeared in comparison.

The snow flew so fast and thickly that the road was one with the land around it. The only things keeping Lydia out of a ditch were the reflectors by the side of the road. She turned on the radio to catch the weather forecast, as if she needed someone to tell her it was snowing. Bryce has been right to insist on a train. His practicality was one of his best qualities. Lydia could never have driven to Bryce's house in the storm. She exhaled with relief to see the sign marking the train station entrance. At last, she had arrived. Everything would be fine.

Almost on cue, her phone dinged. Of course Bryce would have calculated the time she needed to get to the train station and texted accordingly.

Bryce: *Are you there yet?*

Lydia: *Yes, I'm parked and about to walk to the platform.*

Bryce: *Good! See you soon.*

Bryce did everything right, which was a significant difference between him and Marco. Bryce made arrangements and followed them to a T, although Marco would have driven her to the station. Marco's presence was more reassuring. If anything happened, he would be there. Bryce merely arranged things on paper. *No, that's not fair*. Bryce was home with his family. He was going to pick her up from the train station. Nothing was wrong with Bryce or his plans.

The problem was that everything was right about Marco.

Lydia sat in the car, wondering if a relationship with Bryce was what she truly wanted. A holiday party was just one step in their burgeoning relationship, yet it felt like one step off a cliff. She couldn't turn back.

"Don't be ridiculous. Get out of the car and walk up to that platform." Talking to herself didn't speak well for her state of mind, but she laughed and got out of the car, lifted her bag, and walked resolutely to the train platform.

The train pulled into the station. The doors opened, and she stepped into the car. When she found an aisle seat, she hefted her overnight bag onto the rack above her head and sat. *There, that wasn't so hard.*

Anxiety niggled at her, saying, *There's no turning back.*

She tried to ignore it. She experienced the same sort of anxiety at the beginning of each semester. By the end of the first day, she was fine.

No, it's not the same! She got up, grabbed her bag, and stepped out of the train car just as the doors closed behind her. As she headed back to her car, she tried with all her might not to think. Lydia just had a gut feeling. She couldn't rationalize her way around it.

She'd done what she had to do, although she couldn't have explained it to anyone.

Her car was still warm inside, and she started the engine. *Do it now and get it over with.*

"Bryce, it's Lydia."

"Hi! You must be on the train."

"No."

But I thought you were there in the—"

"Bryce, I'm so sorry. I'm not coming."

"But I just called to check. The trains are running just fine."

"I know. It's not the trains. I can't come."

His voice had an edge. "But I told everyone you were coming."

"I know. Bryce, I think you're amazing."

"You're breaking up with me." He sounded stunned.

"I'm sorry. I really tried."

"Does it take that much work?"

"I'm sorry. It shouldn't. It's no reflection on you. I'm just not—"

The call ended. *He didn't just hang up on me.* It had to be the storm.

She couldn't just leave it like that, so she called him again. "Bryce?"

No, he hung up again. So that was it. It was over.

Lydia took in a deep breath and exhaled, feeling as

though she'd just escaped making the worst mistake of her life. She'd nearly yoked herself to someone with whom she had nothing in common. In fact, all that had ever held them together were his feelings for her and her appreciation of his attention. But she didn't return his feelings, and she never would.

Not only would Lydia survive on her own, but she would thrive. She might never have Marco's love, but she would live her life—not Bryce's or anyone else's. If Bryce turned out to be her last chance at a long-term relationship, she would have no regrets. That realization felt like a weight had been lifted. *Hey, Atlas. Could you hold this for me? I've got someplace to go.*

In the half hour she'd been at the station, the snow had turned to sleet and ice. The slick road put her small all-wheel-drive vehicle through its paces. In the midst of the snowy haze thatching in the air, a deer leaped across the road before her. Lydia touched her brakes and started to fishtail but regained control of the car. Out of nowhere, another deer leaped in front of her car, and she managed to miss it, but the sudden maneuver sent her car into a spin. Terrified, Lydia gripped the wheel and tried to right herself. Despite the vibration of the antilock brakes, the car careened off the road and down an embankment.

FIFTEEN

FOR THE SECOND time that evening, Marco asked Mel to cover for him.

"Yeah, sure—if you mean it this time."

"Oh, I mean it." To Theo, he said, "I've got to find Lydia."

"Find her? She's lost?"

"I'll explain later. I've got to go."

"Marco, be careful!"

On his way out the door, Marco said, "I will."

Every bar patron who'd stopped by that evening had talked about the bad weather, though most of them had already gone home. As Marco pulled onto the road, it was even worse than he'd expected. The plows hadn't been through, so it would take him forever to get to the station. The clock on the dashboard told him he had, at the most, five or six minutes to spare, which made his chances of getting there before the train left unlikely. But he was determined. Most sane drivers were already home, so he had the road practically to himself. He was glad his SUV had enough clearance to forge through the rapid accumulation of snow, but he worried about Lydia in her subcompact car. He worried so much that he kept an eye out on the side of the road in case she'd pulled over or gotten stuck.

With no sightings of Lydia's car, Marco was relieved to arrive at the train station entrance. The train was there waiting, so rather than waste time parking, Marco pulled up to the drop-off point and got out. As he ran up the stairs, he called Lydia's name, but the train pulled away before he reached the platform.

He had missed her. Fool that he was—Jack had pegged him correctly—Marco looked behind every pillar, as though she might appear. When that failed, he went back to his car and drove past every car in the parking lot. What he hoped to do once he found her parked car was unclear even to him. Perhaps seeing her car would reinforce the hopelessness of his situation.

He drove around the lot twice before he was convinced. Lydia's car was not there.

Marco pulled out his phone. "Eve? Hi, it's Marco."

"Hi, Marco. How are—"

"Where's Lydia?"

"I thought you knew. She's going to Bryce's. She left for the train station a while ago. The train will have left by now."

"I know." He hesitated to confess. "I'm here at the train station."

"Oh." So much was packed into that single word. It sounded surprised, intrigued, and ultimately sorry for Marco. He could think of no reason to be there that didn't sound pathetic. But Eve was kind enough not to inquire.

"Eve, her car isn't here. I thought maybe she changed her mind and decided not to brave the weather."

"Not that I know of." Eve's voice sounded increasingly tense. "If she'd changed her mind, she would have called me. We always call each other— especially in weather like this." Eve's voice became muffled. "It's Marco. Lydia's missing."

In the background, Dylan said, "Tell him we're leaving right now."

Marco looked out at the whiteout conditions. "Eve, no. The roads are bad. Visibility is close to zero. I'm already out here. I'll look for her."

"Dylan's here with his truck. We're on our way out the door."

It wasn't Marco's place to object. Besides, another two sets of eyes couldn't hurt. "Okay. Keep your phone handy."

"You too."

He pulled out of the train station. She must never have made it to the train station, so he kept his eyes peeled on that side of the road. Barely able to see in the blizzard conditions, he crept along slowly, desperate to find her yet afraid for what he might see when he did.

It was bad enough to lose her to Bryce, but death was unthinkable. Lydia was such a good person. She deserved a full life, even if it had to be with Bryce. With a bitter laugh, he realized that, as usual, Lydia was right. Marco couldn't sustain a relationship, not even with the woman he'd finally realized he loved. It must be some sort of poetic justice—the ladies' man finally fell in love then got dumped. Although you couldn't really be dumped if you had never been together in the first place. So he couldn't even inspire a good poem.

Nearly halfway home, he spotted the faint snow-covered remnants of tire tracks where a car appeared to have skidded off the road.

He pulled over and called Eve. "I found some

tracks skidding off the road on the side going from the station toward town. They're on the wrong side to be Lydia's, but I've got to make a quick stop to see if someone needs help."

Marco backed up to the point where the tracks left the road. The fading dusk and the blowing snow made it almost impossible to see anything. He stood outside of his car and looked down at a roadside embankment. Mounded snow almost concealed the shape of a small car, but a tiny red light blinked above it and drew his attention. He half climbed, half skidded down to the car, where he discovered that the small red light came from a necktie fastened to the antenna. Adrenaline surged in his chest as he climbed through the deep snow to the driver's-side door. He pounded on the window. "Lydia!"

"Marco!" she called through the fogged-up window.

He struggled to open the door, and she pushed from inside. When the ice-encrusted door opened, it threw Marco backward into the snow.

He'd expected to see a lot of things when he found Lydia, none of them good. But he didn't expect to hear her laughing.

She reached down. "Here, let me help you get up."

"Why would I when I can provide you with so much entertainment?"

"I'm sorry. Here, take my hand."

He reached out and pulled her down into the snow with him. They laughed together.

"You scared me," he said.

"I'm okay."

"I thought we'd lost you."

"You haven't lost me."

His lips parted, then Lydia looked up at the road as a truck pulled up behind Marco's car. "Dylan?"

They both stood, and Marco said, "When I didn't see your car at the station, I called your mom."

"Lydia!" Eve started down the embankment.

Lydia called, "Stay there. I'm fine. My car is a little banged up, but…"

"I don't care about the car! You're all that matters!"

"Wait there, Mom. I'm on my way up." She turned back to the car. "I just need my purse and my overnight bag."

"I'll get them. You go up to your mother."

Once everyone was reunited, Eve said, "Hop in the truck. Let's get out of this weather."

Lydia replied, "You two go home. I need to talk to Marco."

That got Marco's attention, but he had no objections.

"Besides, there's more room in his car for my baggage." She turned to Marco. "Do you think you could take me back to the bar and make one of those coffee drinks of yours?"

Puzzled, Marco said quickly, "Sure." His eyes darted toward Eve and Dylan. "The roads will only get worse."

Lydia said, "We need to talk."

Marco nodded slowly. "Okay, but if the snow keeps coming down at this rate, you might find yourself stranded at the brewpub."

Eve and Dylan were noticeably silent, so Marco put Lydia's bag in the back seat then closed Lydia's door.

Dylan said, "We'll follow you as far as the brewpub."

"Mom, text me when you get home."

Minutes later, Marco and Lydia sat by the woodstove. The weather had driven all the pub business away. No one needed to be out in that weather.

Theo said, "I'm closing early. If you need me, I'll be upstairs."

Marco set down two coffee drinks just as Lydia received a text from her mother.

"Mom and Dylan got home safely."

"That's good to hear."

Marco got a blanket from a chest in the corner and wrapped it around Lydia.

With a laugh, she said, "Marco, I'm fine. Really."

While Lydia sipped her drink, Marco watched quietly then said, "Your car was heading in the wrong direction."

She looked into his eyes. "It was the right direction for me."

"Because of the weather?"

She shook her head. "Because of you."

Despite the look in her eyes, he couldn't trust himself to believe what he was hearing.

Lydia continued, "I was on the train, ready to go." She looked into the fire. "Bryce is a really great guy. But he isn't for me. I think I always knew it, but I..."

Marco felt elated until he realized that it didn't change a thing where he was concerned. She could not like them both at the same time.

"I wanted to be loved, and Bryce could have done that. I think we were headed that way. But being loved isn't the same as being in love. And I wasn't—at least not with him. So I got off the train and headed for home." She smiled. "That didn't quite go as planned, but that tie you gave me came in really handy! Apparently, running off the road and going down an embankment can mess up your lights, and the snow was falling so fast that I was afraid no one would find me."

Marco couldn't take his eyes from her. "I should have found you a long time ago."

Lydia eyed him unsurely. "I'm an idiot."

"Is this the part where I'm supposed to look shocked?" He smiled, but it faded. Marco felt nervous. He had never been nervous with a woman. "You've been such a good friend."

"Yeah, well... thanks." She lowered her eyes, looking disappointed, which filled him with hope.

Marco ran a hand through his hair. "But the thing is that things change. I've changed." He found such depth of emotion in her eyes, which shimmered in the firelight. He wondered how long that depth had been there.

"That's why I came back."

"Because you're in love?"

She averted her eyes. "How did you know?"

"Because I love you."

She lifted her eyes to meet his. "I have wanted to hear that."

"Just to clarify, because you love me too?"

"Yes!" She laughed.

Marco's heart felt close to bursting. "Then would you mind putting down that damned coffee drink?"

"Yes—I mean no."

Without waiting, Marco took the drink from her and set it aside. Then he held her face in his hands and kissed her.

The fire crackled and warmed them, while outside, large snowflakes floated down and settled in a thickening blanket. The boats in the harbor seemed to lie atop the frozen, snow-covered sea. A snowstorm at Christmastime was magical when viewed from an indoor fireside, but Marco and Lydia didn't notice any of that, because they were in love.

SIXTEEN

THEY STAYED UP ALL NIGHT, sometimes talking but always curled up together by the woodstove. Warm in each other's arms, they discussed all the moments they'd missed and the ones they would share in the future. All that mattered anymore was that they'd found each other at last and discovered the love they'd had all along. Lights twinkled from the evergreens Lydia and Allie had hung. Christmas magic surrounded them, and love filled their hearts.

Marco pointed at the rafters. "See that?"

Lydia smiled. "Mistletoe."

"Like I needed a hint."

He brushed his lips against hers, and the day dawned on their kiss.

Marco brought over two fresh mugs of coffee then sat with his arm around Lydia's shoulder and stroked her long hair. "This mane of yours changes color in the firelight. It almost looks orange at times, but I think it's mostly red."

Lydia frowned. "Auburn."

He hugged her closer. "I stand corrected."

She rested her head on his shoulder. "I like this. What took us so long to get here?"

"If we have to place blame, I plead guilty."

"I wasn't trying to blame you. I just feel so happy. I wish we could have just known. Why can't there just be a computer pop-up window?"

He pulled back just enough to take a good look at her. "What are you talking about?"

"A window that pops up and says, 'This is the one. This is the person who will make you happy forever.'"

"That would take all the fun out of it."

"I'm not sure I'd call it fun."

"Why? I've had fun since I met you."

Lydia laughed. "That is such a Marco thing to say."

"Hey! What's that supposed to mean?"

"It's easy when you're not in love. That torch I was carrying got pretty heavy."

"I think I was in love, but I just didn't know it." Marco stared at the fire. "I used to think I knew what love was, and I thought I could control when it happened. When I decided I was ready, love would strike like some huge, overpowering sledgehammer of emotion, and I would just know. Apparently, that's not how it works. Love snuck up on me. While I thought I was keeping love on a shelf, ready for when I chose to feel it, it was already there in the things that we shared, like our first coffee at the diner. I think that's when it started. You were different."

Lydia wrinkled her nose. "Thanks."

"No! I mean in a good way. You were smart and interesting, and I wanted to know more about you."

"For me, it was your first crochet chain."

He laughed. "First and last."

Lydia shook her head. "Such a loss to the needlework world."

Marco nodded. "The thing is that the bar customers look at you weird when you set down a granny square to pour someone a drink."

She had an almost-serious expression. "I see what you mean."

Marco's smile faded. "If not our first coffee, maybe it was when we hacked Decker's PowerPoint. You were all in, and I was impressed. And no one cleans a restaurant like you do. That pretty much clinched it."

Her eyebrows drew together. "Your typical epic love story."

"When you accidentally dipped your hair like a paintbrush in the cleaning bucket and I pulled it back and tied it in a knot so it would stay out of the way, you looked so adorable. I could have hugged you right then. But being with you was so effortless that I didn't even know what it was."

With a wistful look in her eyes, Lydia said, "I knew how I felt, though I really tried to be friends."

Marco drew her closer as they looked into the fire. "Those are the first of many moments to come. When I'm old and sitting in my duct-taped recliner with the remote in one hand and a beer in the other—a Silva Brothers' craft beer, of course—I want to have ten thousand moments with you to remember, because that's what love is, and I want it with you."

THEY SPENT much of the morning finding a tow truck driver to retrieve Lydia's car and take it to an auto shop for repair. Then Marco drove her home.

As he walked her to the door, he asked, "Do you know what this is?"

"What *what* is?"

"It's perfect snowball weather."

Lydia kept walking. "I'm sure kids all over Pine Harbor will enjoy it."

"Oh, I'm sure they will."

A snowball hit her back.

"You're kidding."

With a mischievous grin, Marco shook his head.

"Really? Oh, it's on!" Lydia formed a snowball and ran after him. She took her best shot but missed him.

"Aww. Nice try. You get a participation trophy!"

Her eyes widened. "Oh, wow. You have just awoken a sleeping snowman!"

As he taunted her without even bothering to make another snowball, she landed one on his chest that sent flakes flying onto his face and hair. He gave chase and caught her by the waist, and they landed in a freshly plowed pile of snow.

"Be careful. It would be a shame to get snow on that red hair."

"Auburn." She gathered her hair behind her.

"Wait. Hold it right there."

"Why?"

"So I can put this handful of snow down the back of your neck." He grinned deviously.

"You wouldn't dare."

"Oh, yes, I would—unless..."

She tried to wriggle out of his arms. "Unless what?"

"Unless you kiss me."

Her shoulders relaxed, and she turned around. Smiling sweetly, she started to put her arms around his neck, then she pushed his handful of snow into his face and burst into peals of laughter.

Marco laughed, too, and, leaving the melting snow on his face, took hers in his hands and kissed her. She squealed at the coldness of the snow, then she kissed him back.

He brushed snow from her face and said, "Another one to add to the ten thousand memories."

No longer laughing, Lydia put her arms about Marco's neck, and they held one other.

FROM HER UPSTAIRS APARTMENT, Eve gazed out the window. "Lydia's home—with Marco."

Dylan joined Eve and put his arm around her. "Those look like two people in love."

Eve slipped her arm around Dylan's waist and smiled.

SEVENTEEN

The sun set on Christmas Eve at the brewpub. They'd closed early for the holiday, but preparations were afoot for a party. Their circle of friends had all received cryptic social media invitations to "an important holiday event" via personal message. By five o'clock, nearly everyone had arrived.

Caroline asked Theo, "What is this about?"

With a glint in his eye, Theo said, "I'm not at liberty to say."

Kim leaned on the bar. "Oh, come on! It's not nice to keep secrets!"

"It's not my secret to tell."

With a determined expression, Kim looked around and took attendance, counting on her fingers. "Theo and Marco, obviously, since you own the place.

Allie's here, duh, because of Theo. But Allie, Caroline, and I form three-fifths of the lunch gang."

Tilting her head, Caroline asked, "We're a gang now?"

"Is *crew* better? I'm trying out names."

Caroline studied Allie. "You don't look nearly as curious as the rest of us are. You know something."

Allie made a guilty face but said nothing.

Kim asked, "Speaking of the rest of us, where are Eve and Lydia?"

Before anyone could answer, the front door opened, letting in a freezing gust. In walked an unassuming gentleman in a topcoat. He had a thick shock of white hair. Theo rushed over to him and ushered him back to the kitchen.

Kim said, "He's a little overdressed for a cook. And the bar's closed, isn't it?"

Theo returned with the mysterious gentleman, who had dispensed with his overcoat to reveal a wool suit, and led him to the window that looked over the harbor. Then he turned. He already had everyone's attention. "Please sit down."

Two small rows of seats were arranged facing the window. Everyone exchanged curious looks as they took their seats. The next moment, the wedding march played over the sound system.

Theo and Allie emerged from the kitchen

together and stood on either side of the gentleman at the window. Then Dylan and Eve, who had a bouquet in hand, joined them and stood facing the stranger.

The dapper gentleman began, "Dearly beloved, we are gathered here..." and a wedding proceeded. Surprised expressions gave way to a few teary eyes as the minister pronounced Dylan and Eve husband and wife. As he said it, light snow drifted down through the windows behind him.

He'd barely gotten out, "You may now kiss the bride," when Kim leaped to her feet and burst into applause.

Dylan and Eve turned to face everyone. "Surprise!"

As everyone surrounded the newlyweds with well-wishes and questions, Mel took a flute of champagne to each guest.

Dylan said, "We've already waited nineteen years, so we didn't want to wait any longer."

Eve beamed. "Neither of us wanted a big wedding. We considered eloping, but then we thought about all of you. What better way to celebrate being together than with our dear friends? After all, without you, we might not even be here."

Kim made a noise, something between "Oh!" and a sob, and threw her arms about Eve and Dylan. Then she drew in a sharp breath. "Where is the honeymoon?"

Eve answered, "With the holidays, we thought we would wait until later. We don't have any definite plans yet."

Dylan cleared his throat. "Well, that's not quite true."

Eve looked at him, clearly confused.

He set down his champagne and reached into his inside jacket pocket for an envelope, which he then gave to Eve. "Merry Christmas."

Dylan answered her questioning look with a broad smile. She opened the envelope, pulled out an airline ticket, and gasped. "Paris? I've always wanted to go there!"

"I know. Can you wait until April?"

Eve threw her arms around his neck and hugged him, which looked like a fairly strong yes.

The minister reminded them that they needed to sign the wedding license to make it official.

ONCE THE PAPERWORK was dispensed with, Dylan said, "Madame, your carriage awaits."

Allie and Theo brought the newlyweds' coats to them.

Then Marco and Lydia held out a couple of folded blankets. "You'll probably need these too."

They opened the door to find a horse-drawn sleigh. Lydia's jaw dropped. Once they were seated and covered in blankets, the driver gave them each a glass of champagne and took them on a scenic ride around the harbor.

"Merry Christmas, Mrs. Vaughan."

She shook her head, eyes brimming with love. "Mr. Vaughan, Merry Christmas."

EIGHTEEN

The Christmas snow had melted away in an unseasonal thaw, but that didn't dampen the spirits inside the Silva Brothers' Brewpub. Pine Harbor's Christmas had been filled with family and love, even more so than usual. While Eve and Dylan pored over Paris travel brochures, Lydia and Marco took full advantage of being off from school. When Marco wasn't working, they were together. Allie closed up shop for the holiday week and spent most of her time at the brewpub, but work kept Theo so busy that she often helped them out or caught up on her reading.

Theo and Marco had announced a special New Year's Eve party, which had sold out completely. It was in full swing by the time Caroline arrived with a date.

All of their lunch group was there, but Kim was the first to go over and greet her. "Two questions. Who's your friend? And does he have a brother? Okay, maybe three questions. What's the brother's phone number?"

But her questions became irrelevant when Kim paired up with a regular dance partner. During a slow dance, she caught Allie's eye over her dance partner's shoulder and, after pointing at the back of his head, gave him an enthusiastic thumbs-up.

Allie watched Dylan and Eve as they danced. They had finally found each other, and Allie's heart filled with joy to see them together. In anticipation of the honeymoon in Paris, Marco played an Edith Piaf song for them.

The whole evening was so full of love and holiday joy that it was practically perfect. When they rang in the new year, Theo escaped from behind the bar and found Allie. "Happy New Year." He kissed her then said, "I've got a surprise."

As he pulled an envelope out of his pocket, Allie's eyebrows drew together. "This isn't another trip to Paris, is it?"

He laughed. "Sorry, no. And it's not really a present, exactly. I just wanted to show you."

"Okay..."

He unfolded a paper. "It's the deed to the land I once showed you. I bought it."

"Oh, wow! That's fantastic!" She was so happy for him. Theo had been saving for that piece of land on a hill overlooking the harbor for years. He had worked so hard and achieved so much. "Congratulations."

By the end of the evening, Allie was exhausted. She wondered how Theo managed to look so energized. Perhaps his vibrant spirit was what always made the events at the brewpub so fun. The evening had been a tremendous success, but the guests had all gone home. Only their good friends lingered for a last drink. Even Marco and Lydia were off to an after-hours party. Mel finished cleaning up, and Theo locked up after she left. He and Allie were alone.

He took her hand and led her to the window. "I want to show you something."

"It's snowing! Oh, what a nice way to end New Year's Eve!"

Theo smiled. "It is, but it could be better."

Allie couldn't see how. The evening had been a fantastic way to ring in the New Year.

As they stood side by side, looking out at the gentle snow falling peacefully on Pine Harbor, Theo asked, "Do you remember the day we first met?"

She turned to him. "Are you serious?"

He just smiled.

"Yes, I'm pretty sure I can remember how we first met."

"Since then, I might've mentioned that I've fallen in love."

Allie smiled through her confusion. "Yes, once or twice."

"I've been looking forward to having a moment alone."

"Me too." She started to put her arms around him, but he held them to stop her then took her hands in his. "Allie?" He dropped down to one knee and looked up at her.

Allie drew in a sharp breath.

"From the start, you have always surprised me, so I wanted to surprise you this time—although it's no surprise that I love you. Allie Pidgeon, will you marry me?"

"Yes, I will."

A few leftover fireworks went off in the distance, but Theo and Allie barely noticed.

THE KITCHEN DOOR OPENED A CRACK, just enough for Marco and Lydia to peek at the newly engaged couple.

Lydia whispered, "I think she said yes."

Marco nodded. "They look happy. We might have to try that sometime." Then he closed the door gently and drew Lydia into his arms.

THANK YOU!

Thank you, reader. With so many options, I appreciate your choosing my book to read. Your opinion matters, so please consider sharing a review to help other readers.

BOOK NEWS

Would you like to know when the next book comes out? Click below to sign up for the J.L. Jarvis Journal and get book news, free books, and exclusive content delivered monthly.

news.jljarvis.com

ACKNOWLEDGMENTS

Editing by Red Adept Editing
redadeptediting.com

Pine Harbor Series

Allison's Pine Harbor Summer
Evelyn's Pine Harbor Autumn
Lydia's Pine Harbor Christmas

Holiday House Novels

The Christmas Cabin
The Winter Lodge
The Lighthouse
The Christmas Castle
The Beach House
The Christmas Tree Inn
The Holiday Hideaway

For more information, visit jljarvis.com

ABOUT THE AUTHOR

J.L. Jarvis is a left-handed opera singer/teacher/lawyer who writes books. She received her undergraduate training from the University of Illinois at Urbana-Champaign and a doctorate from the University of Houston. She now lives and writes in upstate New York.

Sign up to be notified of book releases and related news:
news.jljarvis.com

Email JL at:
writer@jljarvis.com

Follow JL online at:
jljarvis.com

facebook.com/jljarvis1writer

twitter.com/JLJarvis_writer

instagram.com/jljarvis.writer

bookbub.com/authors/j-l-jarvis

pinterest.com/jljarviswriter

goodreads.com/5106618.J_L_Jarvis

amazon.com/author/B005G0M2Z0

youtube.com/UC7kodjlaG-VcSZWhuYUUl_Q